W9-DAE-284

DATE DUE

OCT 03 OCT 0 6 03 OCT 0 6 03			
97			

SYNNÖVE SOLBAKKEN

WORKS OF
BJÖRNSTJERNE BJÖRNSON

PATRIOTS EDITION

SYNNÖVE SOLBAKKEN

Translated from the Norse

By

RASMUS B. ANDERSON

NEW YORK
DOUBLEDAY, PAGE & COMPANY

BIOGRAPHICAL SKETCH

OF

BJÖRNSTJERNE BJÖRNSON.

Only a very condensed sketch can here be given of the great Norse poet, novelist, dramatist, orator, and political leader, whose works are now offered to the American public.

Björnstjerne Björnson was born December 8, 1832, in Kvikne, a rural district in the central part of Norway, at the foot of the beautiful Dovre Mountains, where his father was a Lutheran priest. The scenery is grand and majestic, though rather austere; and life is of a somewhat solitary character, for the farm-houses here, as elsewhere in Norway, are widely separated from each other.

While the poet was yet a mere boy, his father was transferred to the celebrated Romsdal, one of the finest valleys in Western Norway. Here the sombre hues of the mountain-masses are mingled with the variegated splendor of the valley. Dark fjords stretch their long arms into the country. The mountains, whose summits are crowned with ice and snow, rise almost perpendicularly from the water's edge in

some places, while in others golden fields, green mead-
ows, and fine forests lie between the fjord and the
mountain.   The ravines on the mountain-tops are
filled with mighty glaciers, that clasp their frosty
arms around the valley, and send down, like streams
of tears along the weather-beaten cheeks of the mountains, countless waterfalls and cascades, overarched
by beautiful rainbows, and falling in endless variety
into the valley and fjord below.

The environments are of no slight importance in
the development of genius, and we find the impressions inspired by the weird scenes amid which Björnson spent the days of his childhood, constantly unfold-
ing blossoms in his poems, novels, and dramas.   Nor is
it alone the impressions that these scenes made upon
him that are to be taken into account.   The Norse
folk have been looking upon these same silver-crested
mountains, from which the summer sun never de-
parts, upon the same ocean, islands, lakes, fjords, and
flower-clad valleys, and have listened to the same
melodious brooks, babbling streams, thundering riv-
ers, roaring waterfalls, and soughing groves, for generations.   These surroundings have more or less
colored the Norse myths, epics, folk-lore tales, bal-
lads, melodies, proverbs, eddas, sagas, customs, man-
ners ; in short, all the products of the Norse mind and
heart, the whole life of the Norsemen.   In estimat-
ing Björnson's genius, therefore, the influence of the
environments and of Norse traditions upon countless
generations of his forefathers must not be over

looked. We hope to be understood when we say, briefly, that the external, physical nature of Norway largely modified and moulded the ancient Norsemen's character; that nature and the Norse character thus formed gave color to the Norsemen's religion, tales, traditions, and other intellectual products; that the climate and scenery of Norway, together with the accumulative influence of the national character and the popular traditions and literature upon the people from generation to generation, produced a full-blown flower in the genius of Björnstjerne Björnson; and, finally, that this principle may be applied to any great national writer or artist in any country. Nor do we by this statement mean to exclude the influence exercised by foreign nations and foreign literatures upon Björnson himself, and upon his ancestors.

At the age of twelve Björnson was sent to the Molde grammar school. Molde is a small coast town in Romsdal, which is celebrated on account of the grand and beautiful scenery with which it is surrounded. But he was a dull scholar. When he was admonished to apply himself, in order that he might learn enough to enter the university, he answered, "They want me to study and read so much, while I would prefer to write." He had already begun to think of becoming a poet, and of course the greatest of all poets, though he was constantly reminded that he was thought stupid. People called the boy an agitator. When he was only fifteen years old, he organized a society of boys and founded a paper written by hand. Its name was, as might be expected, "Liberty." In the society political matters were discussed, and Björnson was the leader of the republican party. This was in the year 1848, when revolutionary ideas found their way even to the remotest valleys of Norway. Björnson's society had a debate on the election of president of the French republic, and he voted for Lamartine, while the majority voted for Louis Napoleon.

Nor did Björnson distinguish himself at the university in Christiania, whither he was sent in 1852. He continued to neglect his regular studies, and devoted himself to poetry and journalism. Caring but little for books, he studied all the more earnestly the volumes of nature and human society, both of which he has interpreted with remarkable force and beauty. It is related that a Swede, who visited Christiania in 1853, and was struck by the fine appearance of a young man in a gathering of students, turned to one near him and inquired who that young man was. The answer was, " Björnstjerne Björnson, a young man who wants to become a genius." One of the by-standers, who had listened to the conversation, added, " I would rather call him a young genius who wants to become a man." While pursuing his university course, which he never completed, he produced his first literary work of any considerable length. It was a drama, entitled " Valborg." It was accepted by the managers of the theatre, but, before it was played, he took it back and destroyed it. He had already outgrown it, and decided that it would not do him credit. For some time afterward (1854–56) he devoted his time mainly to dramatic criticism and to reviewing books for "Aftenbladet," later also for "Morgenbladet," and to corresponding for provincial newspapers.

Norway, since her separation from Denmark in 1814, had been striving to create a national literature, and when Björnson entered the university in 1852, the first literary epoch of the young and free nation (the Wergeland-Welhaven epoch) was about being completed. It had produced Maurits Christoffer Hansen, the founder of the Norwegian novel; Johan Welhaven, the leader of the conservative party, which aimed to build up a Norwegian literature on the foundation of foreign, particularly Danish culture; and his great opponent, Henrik Wergeland, under whose banner gathered all the liberal spirits, all who had faith in the ability of Norway to develop an entirely independent national literature, art, and life. Their object was to root out every trace of foreign influence. This first epoch had also produced Asbjörnson and Moe, the collectors of the popular tales of Norway; the great poet, Andreas Munch; the historians, P. A. Munch and Rudolf Keyser; and a considerable number of eminent scholars among whom may be noted Sars the naturalist, Han ten the astronomer, Abel the mathematician, Aasen the linguist and creator of a new language for Norway, based on the dialects. The famous violinist, Ole Bull, also belongs to this epoch, and around him cluster a magnificent group of musical composers, painters, and other artists.

With the beginning of the second half of this century we enter upon the second epoch of modern Norwegian literature — the so - called Björnson - Ibsen epoch. The poets of this period are Björnstjerne Björnson, Henrik Ibsen, Jonas Lie, and Kristofer Janson. Of these Björnson is decidedly the most conspicuous, and may be said to be the legitimate successor to Henrik Wergeland, with whom he has much in common both as poet and political leader. He is in fact carrying forward the work left unfinished by Wergeland; while Welhaven, the great antagonist of Wergeland, has found no eminent successor in the ranks of living Norse writers.

Björnson's literary career really begins with the year 1857, when he published his first novel. Since then his life has been singularly varied and active, and in the midst of his many conflicting occupations he has been an exceedingly prolific writer.

Twice he has been director of a theatre : the first time in 1858, when Ole Bull put the theatre which he had founded in Bergen into his hands ; and the second time in 1865, when the management of the Christiania royal theatre was intrusted to him. He held both positions, however, only for a brief space of time. Three times he has entered the field of journalism ; the first in 1856, as editor of his own paper, the " Illustreret Folkeblad " the second in

1859, as co-editor of "Aftenbladet;" and the third in 1866, as editor and publisher of "Norsk Folke-blad." Since 1856 he has been a constant and diligent contributor to the public press on all questions of national interest. His articles and addresses would alone, if collected, fill many large volumes. His winters he has frequently spent abroad, in Denmark, Germany, France, and Italy, and he is at this writing visiting the United States, whose citizens everywhere give an enthusiastic welcome to the tall, erect, broad-shouldered, and silver-tongued son of the frozen North.

His first novel, produced in 1857, was "Synnöve Solbakken," the volume now presented to our readers in an English dress. It at once made a profound impression, and established his reputation both at home and abroad, not only on account of the simple and charming plot, but also for the short, direct, pithy, saga style in which it was written; and here we may add that the author has been growing increasingly terse and concise in his style from that day to this. It became the corner-stone of a new school of literature, and when we take into consideration that the Wergeland-Welhaven epoch continued to be more or less deeply imbued with Danish culture, modern Norwegian literature may fairly be said to begin with "Synnöve Solbakken." It was the first great national work unimpressed with the old Danish stamp. As is the case in the old Norse sagas, portraits of the characters are not drawn, nor are his works marred by lengthy dissertations from a moral stand-point. Instead of long, fine-spun declamations of this sort, he lets his characters speak for themselves, and leaves it to the reader to judge whether they are good or bad. He does not stop to describe separately the details of features and dress, but he watches his opportunity to give glimpses of them *as the story progresses.* He portrays his men and women while he tells what they do and say, and thus the reader knows, when he has finished the book, how Synnöve, or Thorbjörn, or Aslak must have appeared to the author. As before stated, there has been no interruption in Björnson's literary activity, and he has given the world a series of novels and dramas, which have found their way into all lands and been translated into many tongues. They all reveal a startling psychological insight and acquaintance with the deepest laws of human life. His novels are, besides "Synnöve Solbakken;" "Arne;" "A Happy Boy;" "The Fisher Maiden;" "The Bridal March;" "Magnhild;" "Guiseppe Mansana;" and several short stories. His dramas are: "Halte Hulda;" "Mellem Slagene" (Between the Battles); "Kong Sværre;" "Sigurd Slembe;" "Maria Stuart;" "De Nygifte" (The Honeymoon); "Sigurd Jorsalfar" (Sigurd the Crusader); "En Fallit" (A Bankrupt); "Redaktören" (The Editor); "Kongen" (The King); "Leonarda;" and "Det Ny System" (The New System). His lyric and national songs are published in one volume, and he is also the author of an epic poem, published in a separate vol-

ume, entitled "Arnljot Gelline." When we add to
this a small volume, "Vis Knut" (Wise Knut), and
his little volume " Republiken " (The Republic),
issued late in 1880, we have completed the list of his
published works.

Mr. Björnson is without a peer in the north of
Europe as novelist, national and lyric poet, orator,
and contributor to the daily press ; and as dramatist
he knows but one competitor for the first rank, Henrik Ibsen, whose "Love's Comedy," " Brand," and
" Peer Gynt " Edm. W. Gosse, in his " Studies in the
Literature of Northern Europe" (London, 1879),
characterizes as " a trilogy, perhaps, for sustained
vigor of expression, for affluence of execution, and for
brilliance of dialogue, the greatest of modern times."
On the other hand, it is interesting to notice that
Robert Buchanan, an equally high authority in literature, pronounces Audhild, one of the female characters in " Sigurd Slembe," Björnson's great dramatic
trilogy, " a creation worthy of Goethe at his best," —
worthy, in his opinion, " to rank with ' Clärchen,'
' Marguerite,' and ' Mignon ' as a masterpiece of delicate characterization." Björnson has never been
surpassed in his delineation of delicate female types,
both in his novels and dramas, and this furnishes one
of the best proofs of his claim to rank among the
master poets of any age. Björnson's dramas have
had a boundless influence upon modern thought in
Scandinavia, and we might include Germany, and
when properly translated they will not fail to secure
him the homage of England and America.

It may be said that Björnson's great work, or rather the red thread running through all of Björnson's works, is a struggle for the independence of Norway; an effort to secure an emancipation and development of all those intellectual energies that Norway may properly call her own. We discover this tendency alike in his novels, poems, dramas, and in his miscellaneous writings. He loves his country, and therefore takes a profound interest in every question that concerns its welfare; and it is safe to say that his name is intimately connected with every important issue that has been raised in Norway during the past twenty years. In every question his words and his songs have been heard either *pro* or *con*. In many movements he has been the first who has spoken. His literary works are thoroughly imbued with the progressive spirit of the age. In his novel "Magnhild" and in his drama "Leonarda" he has championed the rights of women and exposed the wrongs in private and domestic life in a manner that would delight the heart of Julia Ward Howe or T. W. Higginson. He saw the corruption of the press and wrote his drama "The Editor." He saw the corruption in the world of trade and commerce, and wrote his drama "The Bankrupt;" a play, by the way, which it seems might be made very successful on the American stage. Presented by an actor like our Barrett, it could not fail to make a powerful impression. In his drama "The King," Björnson has given the fullest and freest expression to his republican tenets. He there represents monarchism as a *lie*, and lets the king himself advocate the republic as the ideal form of government. To those who suggest excuses for and favor the monarchy as a temporary evil, as a necessary school, in which the nation is to be educated and ripened for self-government, he makes the king, who has come to look at his royal position as false and abnormal, address this striking question: "Is it, then, necessary that a people, on their eternal progress toward the truth, should march with a *lie* as their leader?" That a drama enunciating such principles could not be played at the *royal* theatre, needs not to be stated; but those who have embraced the doctrine that all men are created equal and endowed with an inalienable right to life, liberty, and the pursuit of happiness, hail in Björnson the promise of a Norwegian republic. With a keen eye to discover corruption and hypocrisy in the church as well as elsewhere, he has broken many a lance with the priests, and has dealt many a blow to the orthodox bigots of his time.

Björnson's political speeches are landmarks in the national development of Norway; and his lectures are models of eloquence, both as regards style and delivery. One of the most splendid efforts of his life as an orator was his address at Ole Bull's grave, on August 24, 1880, to an audience of more than twenty thousand people. Ole Bull's funeral was more magnificent and solemn than if he had been a king; but the greatest honor of the day was embodied in Björnson's remarks, of which every word was a diamond in the crown of the violinist's immortal fame.

When Björnson writes a national song it is at once taken up and sung by the whole nation, from Lindesnes to North Cape. The national hymn of Norway to-day is his song written in 1859, of which we will attempt to translate two or three stanzas: —

"Yes, we love with fond devotion
    Norway's mountain domes,
Rising, storm-lashed, o'er the ocean,
    With their thousand homes;
Love our country, while we're bending
    Thoughts to fathers grand,
And to saga-night that's sending
    Dreams upon our land.

"Harald Norway's throne ascended
    By his mighty sword;
Hakon Norway's rights defended
    Helped by Öyvind's word;
From the blood of Olaf sainted
    Christ's red cross arose;
From its peaks King Sverre tainted
    Bishops dared oppose.

"Peasants all their axes brightened,
    Ready for each foe;
Tordenskjold in battles lightened
    Set the land aglow.
Even women did assemble
    On the bloody plain;
Others could but weep and tremble,
    But 't was not in vain."

Another very popular song by Björnson is his "Over de höie Fjælde" (Over the Lofty Mountains)

which is very characteristic of the author's style, and
expresses in sublime verses the longings and aspiration
of the young Norsemen. It is, in fact, an expression
of the yearning of the young Norway, and is not in-
applicable to the ambitious struggles of the young
Björnson himself. Mr. Björnson told us, when we
visited him in 1873, that he considered it his best
poem. We are happy to be able to give a spirited
and faithful metrical version of it from the pen of
Auber Forestier, the author of " Echoes from Mist-
land, and translator of Kristofer Janson's " The
Spell-Bound Fiddler," and various other works.

> " Oh, how I wonder what I should see
>   Over the lofty mountains !
> Snow here shuts out the view from me.
> Round about stands the green pine-tree,
>   Longing to hasten over ;
>   Dare it become a rover ?

> " Soars the eagle, with strong wing play,
>   Over the lofty mountains ;
> Rows through the young and vigorous day,
> Sating his courage in quest of prey ;
>   When he will, swooping downward,
>   Tow'rd far-off lands gazing onward.

> " Leaf-heavy apple, wilt thou not go
>   Over the lofty mountains ?
> Forth putting buds 'mid summer's glow,
> Thou wilt till next time wait, I know ;
>   All of these birds art swinging,
>   Knowing not what they 're singing.

> " He who for twenty years long'd to flee
>   Over the lofty mountains,

Nor beyond them can hope to see,
Smaller each year feels himself to be;
　　Hears what the birds are singing,
　　Thou art with confidence swinging.

" Bird, with thy chatt'ring, what wouldst thou here,
　　Over the lofty mountains?
Fairer the lands beyond must appear,
Higher the trees, and the skies far more clear;
　　Wouldst thou but longing be bringing,
　　Bird, but no wings with thy singing?

" Shall I the journey never take
　　Over the lofty mountains?
Must my poor thoughts on this rock-wall break?
Must it a dread, ice-bound prison make,
　　Shutting at last in around me,
　　Till for my tomb it surround me?

" Forth will I! forth!　Oh, far, far away,
　　Over the lofty mountains!
I will be crushed and consumed if I stay;
Courage tow'rs up and seeks the way,
　　Let it its flight now be taking,
　　Not on this rock-wall be breaking!

" One day I know I shall wander afar
　　Over the lofty mountains!
Lord, my God, is thy door ajar?
Good is thy home, where the blessed are;
　　Keep it, though closed a while longer,
　　Till my deep longing grow stronger."

The stirring music written for both of these poems
will be found in the " Norway Music Album," recently published by Oliver Ditson & Co., Boston.

We cannot close this brief sketch of Mr. Björnson
without giving an account of an interesting incident

which occurred in Madison, Wisconsin, during his visit here in the beginning of January, 1881.

While Mr. Björnson was stopping at the hotel in this city, an elderly man came to see him. At the sight of Björnson the man was very much moved, — sobbed like a child, the tears choking his voice, while he attempted to greet the great skald of the North. Mr. Björnson also appeared to be deeply touched by the sudden appearance of his guest, and, grasping his hand, he exclaimed, "Why, are you here, my dear Arne?" The scene of their meeting was intensely affecting, and the reason for it will be evident from the following explanation: [1] Arne is not the "Arne" of Björnson's novel of that name, but Arne Kulterstad, a Norwegian, whose life he had saved twenty years ago. He is a man about fifty years old, has a large frame, and in his younger days must have been the very picture of strength and beauty.

Some twenty-five years ago, Arne, a fine-looking, vigorous young man, who had been a sergeant in the Norwegian army, and as such had become noted for his athletic strength, as well as for his kindly disposition and honest character, had a serious feud with one of his neighbors in his mountain home in Valders, a valley in the central part of Norway. His enemy was a dissipated, mean, cringing, and base villain, who at a party succeeded in getting Arne

---

[1] Mr. Björnson told the story in detail, in my presence, to a reporter of the Madison *State Journal*, from which I have, in part, transcribed it for these pages.

drunk, and persuaded him to sign papers by which he lost his old homestead. The feud grew in bitterness from year to year. One day, when business had brought both to the same place, it came to blows between them, and his foe drew a knife, and gave Arne severe wounds in his hand and arm, the marks of which he bears to this day. There were many other aggravating circumstances, among which may be mentioned, as the worst, the fact that upon the farm which his enemy had gotten possession of Arne's father lived and received his annual allowance, according to Norwegian law. When the father lay upon his death-bed, Arne visited him, and learned that he had been ill-treated, and that his death had probably been hastened by the cruelty of the owner of the farm. This so enraged Arne that revenge was a mere question of time and opportunity. The opportunity was not easily found, for the villain feared Arne, and shrewdly avoided meeting him. He never went out alone. One morning, early, he had, however, deemed it safe to go a short distance from home with his team. But it so happened that Arne too had gone out that morning with his rifle to hunt, when on returning he saw his enemy, and at once determined to give him a mark at least as severe as the one he bore himself. He raised his gun to take sight. He was one of the best marksmen in the country, and had brought down many a bird on the wing; but, unfortunately, as his enemy was walking by the side of his team, he happened to stumble just at the moment when Arne pulled the trigger, and, instead of giving him a severe wound in the arm, as he intended, the bullet entered his breast, and he soon after expired.

Arne was convicted of murder, and sentenced to death. This was in the lower court. The case was appealed. Mark now the remarkable incident which occurred! Having been sentenced to death by this lower court, he was to be transferred to an adjoining bailiwick. The bailiff who had him in charge, knowing his prisoner's honesty and truthfulness, did what probably no other bailiff ever did. The bailiff was very busy, and Arne, knowing this, told him that there was no necessity of his going with him or sending any guards, for he would go alone and place himself in the hands of the officer in the next bailiwick; and such confidence had the bailiff in Arne's uprightness and integrity that he unhesitatingly sent him alone, without any guard, and Arne promptly did as he had agreed!

The sentence of the lower court was confirmed by the supreme court, without any recommendation to pardon. As there was no direct evidence in the case, Arne's lawyer had advised the defendant to deny everything. The effect of a confession was now resorted to, but without avail. He was locked up in prison, and in a few days he was to be beheaded. The young and enthusiastic poet Björnson was at this time in the capital. He had heard of the case, nad read all that had been said about it in the press, and had become so much interested in it that he went to the prison, partly to see this remarkable criminal, partly out of curiosity to see a man who stood at the threshold of execution. He had a long talk with Arne, and was much affected by his manner and by his story of the aggravating circumstances which had led to his great crime. As he was about to leave the prison-cell, Arne arose, stretched out both arms to Björnson, and besought him in tones of deepest agony: "Oh, save me!" These words rang in the ears of the poet, and he determined to move heaven and earth, if this were possible, to procure a pardon. He immediately set himself to work, and wrote for the press what he still considers the most masterly article of his life; indeed, such an article as but few others than Björnson could write. It set the whole community, the whole land, in commotion. The wives and daughters of the judges who had pronounced the sentence and the wives of the members of the king's cabinet were the first to sign a petition to the government for his pardon. The death-sentence was changed by the king to imprisonment for life. For twenty long years Arne had to remain in prison, and not until the summer of 1880 was he released. By this time his wife had died, and his family was scattered. He found himself alone and friendless in a dreary world. After twenty years of confinement within the walls of a prison, liberty itself scarcely seemed a boon. He came to Wisconsin, where he had a married daughter. Hearing of Björnson's arri-

ral in Madison, he immediately came to visit him;
and the meeting of these two men was indeed an
affecting scene. " You are my second father, Björnson, and I cannot tell you how much I love you,"
said Arne to his benefactor. " I owe my life to
you." Arne is poor, and feels nowhere at home.
America seems no place for him. The poet, with his
usual kindness, received him as cordially as a brother.
He offered to care for the unfortunate man in his old
age, and directed me to advance to Arne the necessary funds for defraying his expenses back to Norway, where he will have a home and employment on
Björnson's estate.

This unvarnished tale, besides furnishing a real
Arne by the side of the hero of his novel " Arne,"
gives Björnson a well-earned place among the philan-
thropists of the world.

Of the translation it is needless to say that pains
have been taken to make it as faithful and readable
as possible.

It remains only to be added that in the prepara-
tion of this American edition of Björnson's stories I
have availed myself of the experienced and valuable
assistance of Auber Forestier, whose kind services
are hereby gratefully acknowledged.

RASMUS B. ANDERSON.

MADISON, WIS., *April*, 1881.

SYNNÖVE SOLBAKKEN.

CHAPTER I.

IN a large valley it often happens that there is a high spot, open on every side, which the sun paints with his pencils from early dawn until twilight has faded away. And they who live nearer the foot of the mountains, and seldomer get the sun, call this spot a Solbakke.[1] The person of whom this story tells lived in such a spot as this, and from it the gard[2] took its name. There the snow was last to cover the ground in the autumn, and there it first melted in the spring.

The owners of the gard were Haugians,[3] and were called Readers, because they read the Bible more diligently than other people. The man's name was Guttorm, his wife's Karen. Their first child was a son ; but death took him from them, and for three years they never went

---

[1] A sunny hill.

[2] A Norwegian farm.

[3] Followers of Hans Nielsen Hauge, a Norwegian revivalist in he early part of this century.

on the east side of the church. At the end of
this time a girl was given to them, whom they
named after the boy; his name had been Syvert,
and she was christened Synnöv, as they could
not find anything nearer. But the mother
called her Synnöve, because she had a habit, as
long as the child was small, of adding " mine "
to the name, and so this seemed to come easier.
However this might be, as the girl grew up
every one called her Synnöve, as her mother
did, and most people said that, in the memory
of man, there had not been in the parish so
fair a girl as Synnöve Solbakken. She was
not many years old before they took her with
them to church every Sunday there was service, although at first Synnöve knew no better
than to think the priest was standing there
scolding at Slave Bent, whom she saw sitting
right down below the pulpit. Her father, however, wanted her to go with them, — " to form
the habit," he said ; and her mother wished
it, too, " because no one knew how the child
would be taken care of at home while they were
gone." If there chanced to be a lamb, a kid,
or some little pig on the gard that did not
thrive, or a cow that anything was the matter
with, it was always given over into Synnöve's
possession ; and the mother seemed to feel sure

that from that moment it did well. The father did not quite believe this to be the cause; but " after all it did not matter which of them owned the beasts, so that these only prospered."

On the opposite side of the valley, and close to the foot of a high mountain, there was a gard named Granliden,¹ so called because it lay in the midst of a great spruce forest, the only one for many miles around. The owner's great-grandfather had been among those who lay in waiting for the Russians in Holstein, and from that expedition he had brought home in his knapsack many foreign and strange-looking seeds. These he planted round about his house; but in the course of time one kind after another had died out; meanwhile some spruce cones, which, oddly enough, had been mixed in with the rest, had produced a dense forest, which now shaded the house on every side. The Holstein soldier's name had been Thorbjörn, after his grandfather; that of his eldest son Sæmund, after his father; and thus the owners of the gard had alternately been named Thorbjörn and Sæmund, from time out of mind. But it was said that only every other man at Granliden had good luck, and it was not he who bore the name Thorbjörn. The present owner, Sæ

¹ The spruce slope.

mund, had thought the matter over from various points of view, when his first son was born, but scarcely liked to break the family custom, and so called him Thorbjörn. He pondered much upon whether the boy might not be so brought up that he would escape the fate gossip had laid in his way. He was not altogether sure, but he *thought* he detected a willful disposition in the boy. "That shall be plucked out," said he to the mother; and when Thorbjörn was only three years old the father would sometimes sit with the switch in his hand, and compel him to carry all the sticks of fire-wood back to their place; to pick up the cup he had thrown down; to stroke the cat he had pinched. But the mother preferred to leave the room when the father was in this mood.

Sæmund was surprised to find that the older the boy grew the more there was to correct in him, and this in spite of the fact that he was dealt with more and more strictly. He set him early to reading, and took him out in the fields with him in order to have an eye upon him. The mother had a large house and small children; she could do no more than caress and admonish him every morning, while she was dressing him, and talk gently with the father when Sabbaths brought them together. But Thor-

björn, when he got a whipping because *a-b*
spelled *ab*, and not *ba*, and because he was not
allowed to administer the rod to little Ingrid,
as his father did to him, thought, " It is strange
that I must have such a hard time, while all my
little brothers and sisters have everything so
nice."

As he passed most of his time with his father,
and did not dare say much to him, he talked
little, but thought the more. Once, though,
while they were hauling in the wet hay, the
words escaped him, —

" Why is all the hay dry and in over there
at Solbakken, while here it is still wet ? "

" Because they have the sun oftener than we."

This was the first time he had noticed that
the bright sunshine over there, which he so
many times had sat and looked at with pleas-
ure, was something that he was shut out from.
After that day his eye fell oftener on Solbakken than before.

" Do not sit gaping there," said his father,
and gave him a push. " Over here we have to
drudge all we can, both old and young, if we
are to get anything housed."

Sæmund changed his servant-boy when Thor
björn was about seven or eight. Aslak was the
name of the new servant, and he had already

been about a good deal, though he was yet a
mere boy. The evening he came Thorbjörn
had gone to bed; but the next day, as he sat
reading, the door was pushed open with a kick,
the like of which he had never heard before. It
was Aslak, who came rushing in with a large
armful of wood, and flung it down with such
force that the sticks flew in every direction.
Then he jumped up and down to stamp the
snow off of him, and with every jump he exclaimed, —

"It is cold, said the troll-bride, as she sat in
ice up to her waist!"

The father was not in, but the mother swept
together the snow and carried it out, without a
word.

"What are you staring at?" said Aslak to
Thorbjörn.

"Not at anything," said the latter, for he
was frightened.

"Have you seen the rooster you have in the
back of your book there?"

"Yes."

"He has a lot of hens around him when the
book is shut; have you seen that?"

"No."

"Well, then, look."

The boy did so.

"You are a dunce!" said Aslak to him. But from that moment no one had the power over him that Aslak had.

"You do not know anything," said Aslak, one day, to Thorbjörn, who was trotting after him, as usual, to watch what he was doing.

"Yes, I do. I know as far as the fourth part in my catechism."

"Pooh! No, you have not even heard of the troll who danced with the girl until the sun rose, and then burst like a calf that has been eating sour milk!"

In all his days, Thorbjörn had never heard any one display so much knowledge at once.

"Where was that?" he asked.

"Where? Why, it was — yes, it was over there at Solbakken!"

Thorbjörn stared.

"Did you ever hear of the man who sold himself to the devil for a pair of old boots?"

Thorbjörn forgot to answer, so astonished was he.

"I suppose you are thinking of where that was, hey? It was also over there at Solbakken, right down there in that brook which you see. Lord help us! Your religious knowledge does not amount to much," added he. "I fancy you have not even heard of Kari, with the wooden petticoat."

No, Thorbjörn had not heard of anytning.
And while Aslak was working fast he was tell-
ing still faster, and it was about Kari with the
wooden petticoat, about the mill that ground
salt at the bottom of the sea, about the devil
with the wooden shoes, about the troll that got
his beard caught in the branch of a tree, about
the seven green maidens who pulled the hair out
of Peter Hunter's legs while he slept and could
not possibly awaken; and it all took place over
there at Solbakken.

"What, in the name of Heaven, ails the
boy?" said the mother, the next day. "He
has been on his knees on the bench yonder,
looking over at Solbakken, ever since it was
light."

"Yes, he keeps very busy to-day," said the
father, who lay taking his rest the long Sunday.

"Oh, folks say that he has captured Synnöve
Solbakken," Aslak was saying; "but folks say
so many strange things," added he.

Thorbjörn did not exactly understand him
but nevertheless his whole face grew fiery red.
When Aslak commented on this, he crept down
from the bench, took his catechism, and seated
himself to read.

"Yes, you may as well console yourself with
the word of God," said Aslak; "you will never
get her, any way."

When the week was so far advanced that he thought they had forgotten this, he asked his mother, quite softly, for he felt bashful about it, —

"Say, who is Synnöve Solbakken?"

"She is a little girl who will one day own Solbakken."

"Has she, then, not a wooden petticoat?"

The mother looked at him in surprise. "What is that you say?" said she.

He felt that he must have said something stupid, and was silent.

"A prettier child has never been seen than she is," added the mother, "and that is her reward from the Lord because she is always kind and good and is an industrious reader."

Now he knew that, too.

One day, when Sæmund had been out in the field with Aslak, he said in the evening to Thorbjörn, —

"You must not go with Aslak any more."

But Thorbjörn gave little heed to this. So after a while the order came : —

"If you are found with him any more, it will not be well for you!"

Then Thorbjörn stole after Aslak, when the father did not see him. Sæmund surprised them, though, one day, when they sat talking

3

together; then Thorbjörn got a thrashing, and was told to go in. But afterward Thorbjörn watched his chance to be with Aslak when his father was not at home.

One Sunday, while the father was at church, Thorbjörn got his hands into mischief at home. Aslak and he were throwing snow-balls at each other.

"Oh, stop! you are choking me!" begged Thorbjörn. "Let us throw together at something else."

Aslak was ready at once, and so they threw first at the slender spruce over by the store-house, then at the store-house door, and finally at the store-house window.

"Not at the window itself," said Aslak, "but at the frame around it." Meanwhile, Thorbjörn hit the window-pane, and turned pale.

"Pooh, who will know it? Try it again."

He did so, but hit another.

"Now I will not throw any more," said he.

At that moment his eldest sister, little Ingrid, came out.

"Throw at *her*, Thorbjörn!"

Thorbjörn did so immediately. The girl cried, and the mother came out. She bade him stop.

"Throw, throw!" whispered Aslak.

Thorbjörn was hot and excited ; he did so.

"Why, you must be losing your senses!" said the mother, and rushed toward him, — he ran before, she after, all round the grounds. Aslak laughed and the mother scolded. She caught Thorbjörn at last in a snow-drift, and began to give him a good drubbing.

"I will strike back again, I will!" said he. "That is the way they do here."

The mother ceased in surprise, and looked at him.

"That some one else has taught you," she then said, and taking him silently by the hand, led him in. She spoke not another word to him, but kindly cared for his little brothers and sisters, and told them their father would now soon come home from church. Then it began to grow pretty hot in the room. Aslak asked leave to visit a relative ; he got it at once; but Thorbjörn felt much smaller when Aslak was gone. He had a terrible pain in his stomach, and his hands were so clammy that they made his book moist when he took hold of it. If only his mother would not say anything to his father, when he came home; but Thorbjörn could not bring himself to ask it. Everything his eye fell on kept changing looks, and the clock said, Spanking, spanking, — spanking,

spanking. He had to get up to the window
and look over at Solbakken. It alone, all covered with snow, lay quiet and sparkling in the
sunshine, just as usual; the house stood and
laughed out of all the window-panes, and there
was surely not one of them broken; the smoke
rose with such tremendous joy from the chim-
ney that he judged that over there, too, they
were getting dinner for the church people. No
doubt Synnöve was watching for her father,
and was not to have a whipping when he got
home. Thorbjörn did not know what to do
with himself, and all at once became so affec-
tionate to his sisters that there was no end to
it. To Ingrid he was so good that he gave her
a bright button he had received from Aslak.
She put her arms about his neck, and he put
his arms about hers, saying, —

" Dear little Ingrid mine, are you angry with
me ? "

" No, little Thorbjörn ! You may throw as
much snow at me as you like."

But there was some one stamping the snow
off in the hall. Yes, sure enough, it was the
father. He appeared to be in a good humor,
and that made the matter still worse.

" Well ? " said he, looking around, — and it
was astonishing that the clock did not tumble

down. The mother put the dinner on the table.

" How have things been going here ? " asked the father, as he seated himself and took up his spoon.

Thorbjörn looked at his mother until the tears came into his eyes.

" Oh — well," said she, with incredible slowness ; and she meant to say more, — that he plainly saw. " I gave Aslak permission to go out," said she.

" She did not do it this time," thought Thorbjörn. He began to play with Ingrid, as though he were thinking of nothing else in the world. The father had never taken so long to eat his dinner, and Thorbjörn set to work, at last, to count every bite ; but when he came to the fourth he wanted to see how many he could count between the fourth and the fifth, and then he lost track of it. Finally, the father rose and went out. The window-panes ! the window-panes ! kept ringing in his ears, and he looked round to see whether those in the room were whole. Yes, they were all whole. But now his mother also went out. Thorbjörn took little Ingrid in his lap, and said, so gently that she stared at him in amazement, —

" Come, let us two play the gold princess in the meadow."

That she would like to do. And so he sang while his legs trembled under him : -

"Little blossom,
  Meadow blossom,
  Hearken now to me !
  If you will be my sweetheart so true,
  A velvet cloak I 'll give to you,
  Adorned with gold
  And pearls untold.
  Ditteli, dutteli, deadow, —
  The sun now shines on the meadow ! "

Then she answered, —

"Gold princess,
  Jewel princess,
  Hearken now to me !
  I 'll never be your sweetheart so true,
  I 'll have no velvet cloak from you,
  Adorned with gold
  And pearls untold.
  Ditteli, dutteli, deadow, —
  The sun now shines on the meadow ! " [1]

But just as this game was well under way, his father came in, and fixed knowing eyes on him. Thorbjörn drew Ingrid closer up in his lap, and did not fall from his chair.

The father turned away, said nothing. Half an hour passed; he had not yet said anything, and Thorbjörn was almost about to be happy but did not dare. He knew not what to think when the father himself helped to undress him

[1] Aaber Forestier's translation.

he began gradually to tremble again. Then his father patted him on the head and stroked his cheek ; this he had not done as far back as the boy could remember, and therefore Thorbjörn grew so warm about his heart and over his whole body that fear melted off him like ice beneath a sunbeam. He did not know how he got into bed, and as he could take neither to singing nor shouting, he folded his hands, said Our Father six times forwards and backwards, quite softly, and felt, as he fell asleep, that there was no one on God's green earth he loved so dearly as his father.

The next day he awakened in a terrible fright, because he could not scream ; for he was now to have a thrashing, after all. When opened his eyes, he became aware, to his great relief, that he had only dreamed it ; but soon also became aware that some one else was just about to have a thrashing, and that was Aslak. Sæmund was pacing the floor, and Thorbjörn well knew that step. The rather short but square-built man looked now and then from under his bushy brows in such a way at Aslak that the latter felt plainly what was in the wind ; Aslak was perched on the top of a great barrel, from the side of which his legs now dangled, now were drawn up. As usual, he

had his hands in his pockets and his cap drawn
down lightly on his head, so that the matted
locks of thick black hair protruded from under
the fore-piece. The little crooked mouth was
more crooked than ever ; he held his whole
head slightly aslant, and looked sideways at
Sæmund from beneath his half-closed eyelids.

"Yes, that boy of yours is bad enough,"
said he ; "but, worse still, your horse is troll-
scared."

Sæmund paused. "You are a fool!" said
he, so that it rang through the room, and Aslak drew his eyelids more closely than ever
together.

Sæmund strode on again; Aslak sat still a
while.

"I tell you he is troll-scared," repeated he,
and stole a glance after him to see what effect
that had.

"No ; but he is woods-scared, — that is what
he is," said Sæmund, moving on. "You felled a
tree over him in the field, you careless slouch,
and that is why no one can get him to pass
there quietly any more."

Aslak listened to this a while.

"Well, believe so, if you choose. It is no
disgrace to believe a thing. But I doubt if
that will set your horse right again," he added,

at the same time drawing himself farther back on the barrel, and shading his face with one hand. Sæmund came right over to him, and said in a low, but rather dismal tone, —

" You are a wicked —— "

" Sæmund ! " was heard from the hearth. It was Ingebjörg, his wife, who sat there hushing him as she had hushed the youngest child, who was frightened, and had wanted to scream. The child had been quieted before, and now Sæmund, too, was silent ; but he stuck his fist, which was a very small one for such a square-built man, right up under Aslak's nose, and held it there a while, as he bent forward and fairly scorched the boy's face with his eyes. Then he walked on as before, bestowing on him every now and then a hasty glance. Aslak was very pale, but he laughed over at Thorbjörn with one half of his face, while he kept the half turned toward Sæmund very straight.

" Lord grant us good patience ! " he ex claimed, after a little while ; but at the same time he drew up his elbow, as though to ward off a blow. Sæmund stopped suddenly, and shrieked at the top of his voice, as he brought his foot down on the floor, so that Aslak was completely silenced, —

" Do not *you* dare name *Him !* "

Ingebjörg arose with the infant, and took
Sæmund gently by the arm. He did not look
at her, but still he let his arm drop. She went
to her seat; he walked to and fro once more,
but neither said anything. As this lasted a
while, Aslak had to break the silence again : —

"Aye, He has a great deal to do at Granliden, — that He has!"

"Sæmund! Sæmund!" whispered Ingebjörg,
but before the words reached him Sæmund had
already rushed at Aslak, who thrust out his
foot. It was pushed down, the fellow seized
by it and his jacket collar, lifted up, and then
set against the closed door with such violence
that the panel gave way, and he went through
it head foremost. The wife, Thorbjörn, and all
the children screamed and begged for him, and
the whole house was in one wail. But Sæmund
darted out after him, not remembering to open
the door properly, but kicking the remainder
aside, seized him again, carried him through
the passage out into the yard, raised him high
in the air, and flung him down again with all
his might. And when Sæmund perceived that
there was too much snow for him to be hurt
badly enough, he planted his knee on Aslak's
breast and beat him right in his face, lifted
him the third time, bore him to a place that

was more free from snow, like a wolf that is
dragging after him a dog he has been tearing
to pieces, let him fall again, and this time more
savagely than before, then sprang on him with
his knees; and no one knows how it might
have ended had not Ingebjörg rushed between
with the infant in her arms.

" Do not bring ruin upon us ! " she shrieked.

A while later Ingebjörg sat in the family
room ; Thorbjörn was dressing; the father was
pacing the floor once more, and only paused
now and then to drink a little water, but his
hand shook so that the water flew over his head
and splashed on the floor. Aslak did not come
in, and presently Ingebjörg made a movement
to go out. " Stay in," said Sæmund, as though
it were not to her he was speaking ; and she
stayed in. But a little later he went out himself. He did not come in again. Thorbjörn
took his book and read incessantly, without
looking up, although he did not understand a
single sentence.

A little later in the forenoon the house was
in the old order, although every one had a feel-
ing as though strangers had been visiting them.
Thorbjörn ventured to go out, and the first person he met outside the door was Aslak, who had
packed all his things on a sled; but the sled

was Thorbjörn's. Thorbjörn stared at him; for he looked ugly. The blood had dried on his face, and was smeared all over; he coughed and clutched often at his breast. He looked for a moment silently at Thorbjörn, and then he burst out violently, —

"I do not like your eyes, boy!"

With this he got astride of the sled, seated himself, and started down the hill.

"You can get your sled back where you can find it!" said he, and laughed, as he turned once more and stuck out his tongue at him. Thus departed Aslak.

But during the week that followed the lensmand[1] made his appearance at the house; the father was sometimes absent; the mother wept, and she also was away several times.

"What is it, mother?"

"Oh, Aslak is the cause of it all!"

One day they caught little Ingrid, as she sat and sang: —

> "O blessed world, I am weary
> Now of thy doings so dreary!
> Once the girl puts foot in sight,
> Reason leaves the boy outright;
> Wat'ry food the housewife makes,
> Ease her lazy husband takes;
> Puss beyond the rest is keen and wily,
> For cream she's stealing so slyly." [2]

[1] Bailiff.

[2] Auber Forestier's translation.

There was of course a query as to whom she could have learned this snatch of a song from. As was expected, it proved to be from Thorbjörn. He became much alarmed, and said he had learned it from Aslak. He was then made to understand that if he sang any more such verses himself, or taught them to his sister, he would get a whipping. Shortly after this little Ingrid happened to swear. Thorbjörn was again called up, and Sæmund thought he might as well give him a taste of the rod now; but he cried and made such fair promises for himself that he was allowed to escape this time.

The next Sunday there was service, his father said to him, "You will not have any chance to get into mischief at home to-day; you are going with me to church."

CHAPTER II.

THE church stands, in the peasant's fancy, on a lofty eminence, apart by itself, consecrated to peace, with the solemnity of the grave about it, and the cheerfulness of the mass within. It is the sole house in the valley upon which he has bestowed any ornamentation, and its spire, therefore, actually reaches up a little farther than it appears to reach. Its bells greet him on his way thither, of a bright Sunday morning, and he always uncovers his head to them, as though he would return with thanks their greeting! There is a covenant between him and them which no one can fully estimate. Early in life he doubtless stood by the open door and hearkened to them, while the church people moved past in silent procession down on the road; his father was getting ready, but he himself was too small to go. He combined then many ideas with those heavy, sonorous tones which reigned supreme among the mountains for an hour or two, reëchoing from one to the other; but *one* was inseparably connected therewith clean, new clothes, gay-clad women, and well-groomed horses, with bright harnesses.

And when these bells ring thus one Sunday over his own happiness; when in brand-new, but too large, clothes he walks with dignified assurance by his father's side, on his way to church for the first time, aye, then there is exultation in them. Then, surely, they can fling open all the doors to what he is going to see. And on the way home, when they still keep up their clanging over his head, rocking the singing, the mass, the words of the sermon, in their reverberations, there is chased back and forth what engrossed the eye during the service, — the altar-piece, the costumes, the people; then, once for all, they arch over the previously gathered impressions, and consecrate the smaller church which henceforth he bears within him.

When a little older, he has to tend the herds on the mountains, but of a fine, dewy Sunday morning, as he sits on the stone, with the cattle below him, and listens to the church-bells rising above the tinkle of their bells, he grows melancholy. For there rings through them something bright, cheerful, alluring, from down below: thoughts of acquaintances at church; of the joy when one is there, and the still greater joy, when one has been there, of the good dinner at home; of father, mother, brothers, and sisters; of the merriment on the green in the glad Sunday evening,—and the little heart rebels within his breast. But it always ends with the thought that those were the church-bells that were ringing. He reflects a little, and finds stored away in his mind a fragment of some hymn he has learned; this he sings, hands folded, and eyes peering far down into the valley below, repeats a little prayer, besides, springs up, feels happy, and blows such a blast on his loor that it resounds through the mountains.

Here in the little mountain valley the church has its special language for each age, its peculiar look to each eye; much may have been built up between the individual and it, but never anything over it. It stands full-grown and ready, in the eyes of the candidate for confirmation, with finger pointing upward, half threatening, half inviting, for the youth whose choice is made; broad-shouldered and strong over the sorrows of manhood; with plenty of room and full of tenderness for weary old age. During divine service, young children are brought in and baptized, and it is well known that during this act the devotion is greatest.

Therefore, it is impossible to describe Norse

peasants, corrupted or uncorrupted, without coming into contact at one point or other with the church. There will seem to be a dull uniformity in this; but it is, perhaps, not of the worst sort. Let this be said once for all, and not especially on account of the church visit which here follows.

Thorbjörn rejoiced at the thought of the walk to church and the sights he was to see; his eyes were dazzled with the manifold colors without the church; he felt the weight of the stillness which hung over everybody and everything within before the mass began; and although he did not remember to bow his head himself when the prayer was read, it seemed as though it were bowed by the sight of many hundred bowed heads. The singing began, and all sang at once around him, so that it almost appalled him. So absorbed did he sit there that he started up as from a dream when their pew door was softly opened for some one who came in. After the singing was over the father took this new-comer by the hand, and asked, —

" Is all well at Solbakken? "

Thorbjörn raised his eyes; but whatever he saw, or did not see, there was little connection to be traced between this man and any kind of witchcraft. He was a gentle-looking, fair-com-

4

plexioned man, with large blue eyes, a high
brow, and he looked tall in his seat; he smiled
when he was spoken to, and said " yes " to
every remark Sæmund made, but was, on the
whole, a man of few words.

" If you look over there you will see Synnöve," said the father, as he stooped down to
Thorbjörn, took him on his knee, and pointed
over to the pew opposite, on the women's side.
There was a little girl kneeling on the bench
and looking over the railing. She was still
fairer than the man, — so fair that he had
never seen her equal. She had a red streamer
to her cap, light yellow hair beneath this, and
now smiled at him, so that for a long time he
could not see anything but her white teeth.
She held a shining hymn-book in one hand, and
a folded orange-colored silk handkerchief in the
other, and was now amusing herself by striking the handkerchief on the hymn-book. The
more he stared, the more she smiled ; and now
he chose also to kneel on the bench, just as
she was doing. Then she nodded. He looked
gravely at her a moment, then he nodded. She
smiled and nodded once more ; he nodded again,
and once more, and still once more. She smiled,
but did not nod any more, for a little while,
until he had quite forgotten it; then she nod
ded.

" I want to see, too!" he heard behind him,
and at the same moment felt some one pull him
by the legs to the floor, so that he came near
falling; it was a thick-set little fellow, who now
scrambled valiantly up into Thorbjörn's place.
He, too, had light, but bristling hair, and a
snub-nose. Aslak had probably taught Thorbjörn how the bad boys he met at church and
school should be dealt with. Thorbjörn therefore pinched the boy in return so hard that he
wanted to scream, but did not, and crawled instead very quickly down from the bench, and
seized Thorbjörn by both ears. The latter
made a grab at his hair, and pulled him down
under himself; still the boy did not scream, but
bit Thorbjörn in the thigh. Thorbjörn drew it
back, and dashed the boy's face right against
the floor. Then he was himself seized by the
jacket-collar, and lifted up as though he were a
bag full of straw; it was his father, who took
Thorbjörn on his lap.

" If it were not in church, you would get
a thrashing!" he whispered in his ear, and
squeezed his hand so that it hurt clear down in
his foot. He remembered Synnöve, and looked
over at her; she was still there on her knees,
out was staring before her with such a vacant
look that he began to realize what he had done,

and that it must be something very wrong. As
soon as she noticed that he was looking at her
she crept down from the bench, and was no
more to be seen.

The chorister came forward, and then the
priest; he listened to and watched them closely.
Again the chorister came forward, and again the
priest; but still he sat on his father's knee, and
thought, "Will she not soon look up again?"
The little fellow who had dragged him down
from the bench sat on a foot-stool, farther up
in the pew, and every time he wanted to rise
he got a thrust in the back from an old person, who sat and nodded, but awakened regu-
larly every time the child made a move to rise.
"Will she not soon look up again?" thought
Thorbjörn; and every red ribbon he saw stirring round about reminded him of the one she
wore, and every flashy painting in the old
church was either just as large as, or a little
smaller than, she. Yes, now she stretched up
her head; but as soon as she saw him she
gravely drew it down again. Once more the
chorister came forward, and once more the
priest; the bell was rung, and every one arose.
The father talked again in a low tone to the
fair-complexioned man; they went together
over to the pew where the women were, who

had already arisen.   The first person who came
out from there was a fair-complexioned woman,
who smiled as the man did, but more faintly ;
she was rather small and pale, and held Synnöve by the hand.   Thorbjörn went right over
to the latter ; but she went quickly away from
him, round her mother's dress.

"Let me alone ! " said she.

" This little boy has never been at church
before," said the fair woman, and laid her hand
on him.

" No, and that is the reason why he got to
fighting the first time," said Sæmund.

Thorbjörn looked bashfully up at her, and
then at Synnöve, who seemed to him graver than
ever.   They all went out, — the older ones in
conversation, but Thorbjörn following Synnöve,
who drew closer to her mother whenever he approached her.   The other boy he saw no more.
Outside of the church they paused, and began
a longer conversation.   Thorbjörn several times
heard Aslak named, and as he feared they might
talk a little about him also, at the same time, he
retreated a few steps.

" This is not for you to hear !" said Synnöve's
mother to her.   " Go away a little, my dear; go
away, I say."

Synnöve drew lingeringly back.   Thorbjörn

then went nearer her, and looked at her, and she looked at him; and thus they stood for a long while, just looking at each other. Finally she said, —

" Fy ! "

" Why do you say fy ? " asked he.

" Fy ! " said she once more. " Fy ! For shame ! " she added.

" Why, what have I done ? "

" You have been fighting in church, and while the priest stood there saying mass. Fy ! "

" Yes, but that was a long time ago."

This made an impression on her, and she said presently, —

" Are you the boy whose name is Thorbjörn Granliden ? "

" Yes ; and is it you they call Synnöve Solbakken ? "

" Yes. I have always heard that you were such a good boy."

" No, *that* is not true; for I am the worst one of all of us at home," said Thorbjörn.

" Well, I have never heard " — said Synnove, and clasped her small hands. " Mother, mother he says " —

" Hush ! Be quiet, and go away ! " met her from that quarter, and she paused, then went slowly and backwards to her place, her large blue eyes fixed on her mother.

" I have always heard that *you* were good,"
said Thorbjörn.

" Yes, that may be sometimes when I have
been reading," she replied.

" Is it true that you have such a lot of nisses
and trolls and other bad things over your way ? "
asked he, placing his hands on his sides, with
one foot thrust forward, and resting on the
other, just as he had seen Aslak do.

" Mother, mother ! Do you know what he
says ? He says " —

" Let me alone ! Do you hear ? And do
not come here before I call you ! "

She had to retreat again, slowly and backwards ; as she did so she put a corner of her
handkerchief in her mouth, bit it hard, and
pulled at it.

" Is it not true at all that every night there
is music inside of the hills over there ? "

" No ! "

" Have you never seen trolls, then ? "

" No ! "

" But, in the name of Jesus " —

' Fy ! You must not say that ! "

" Oh, pshaw ! — that is nothing ! " said he,
spitting between his teeth to show how far he
could spit.

" Yes, it is," she replied ; " for if you talk so
vou will go to hell."

"Do you think so?" asked he, decidedly more humble; for he had only thought that he might get a whipping for it, and his father was now standing so far away. "Who, for instance, is the strongest over your way?" asked he, and pushed his cap a little more to one side.

"I am sure I do not know."

"Well, over our way it is father. He is so strong that he thrashes Aslak; and Aslak is strong, I can tell you."

"Ah, indeed!"

"Once he lifted a horse."

"A horse?"

"Yes; that is as true, as true — for he told me so himself."

Then she could have no doubts, either.

"Who is Aslak?" asked she.

"He is a very bad boy, I can assure you. Father whipped him so hard that in the whole world there never was any one whipped so hard before."

"Do you fight over there at your house?"

"Yes, sometimes, when — Do not you do so over at your house?"

"No, never."

"What do you do there, then?"

"Oh, mother gets the meals ready, knits, and

sews; Kari does these things, too, but not as
well as mother, for Kari is so lazy. But Randi
takes care of the cows; father and the boys work
out in the field, or else keep busy at home."
This seemed to him a satisfactory explanation.
"Then every evening we read and we sing," she
continued, "and we do so on Sundays, too."

"All of you?"

"Yes."

"That must be tedious."

"Tedious? Mother, he says"— but then
she remembered that it was forbidden her to
bother her mother. "Oh, you had better believe I own ever so many sheep," said she.

"Do you?"

"Yes. Three of them are going to have
lambs this winter, and one of them, I am quite
sure, will have two."

"And so you have sheep, have you?"

"Yes; and I have cows and pigs, too. Have
you none?"

"No."

"If you will come over to see me, you shall
have a lamb. Then you will surely get more
from it."

"That would be too nice for anything."

They were silent for a while. "Cannot Ingrid have a lamb, too?" asked he.

" Who is Ingrid ?"

" Why, Ingrid, — little Ingrid."

No, she did not know her.

" Is she smaller than you ? "

" Yes, of course she is smaller than I, — just about like you."

" Oh, dear me ! You must bring her along do you hear ? "

Yes, he would do so.

" But," said she, " if *you* get a lamb, *she* can have a pig."

This he, too, thought was far wiser; and then they talked a little about their common acquaintances, of whom, to be sure, they had not many. Their parents were now ready, and they must go home.

That night he dreamed about Solbakken, and he thought he saw only white lambs over there, and a little fair girl with red ribbons in the midst of them. Ingrid and he talked every single day about going to Solbakken. They had so many lambs and little pigs to tend that they knew not which way to turn among them. Meanwhile, they wondered greatly that they could not go over there at once.

" Just because that little girl asked you ? ' said the mother. "Did you ever hear the like ! '

" Never mind ; you just wait till the nex⁴

Sunday there is service," thought Thorbjörn,
"and then you shall see."

It came.

"You are said to be so bad about boasting
and lying and swearing," said Synnöve to him,
"that you cannot be allowed to come until you
have stopped your bad habits."

"Who says so?" asked Thorbjörn, surprised.

"Mother."

Ingrid waited in suspense for his coming
home, and he told her and the mother what
had happened.

"Now you see!" said the mother. Ingrid
said nothing; but after this both she and the
mother reminded him every time he swore or
boasted. Ingrid and he, meanwhile, fell into a
quarrel about whether "the dog take me" was
swearing or not. Ingrid got a whipping, and
after that he kept using "the dog take me" the
whole day. But toward evening his father
heard it. "Yes, he shall take you!" said he,
and gave him a blow that sent him reeling.
Thorbjörn felt most ashamed before Ingrid, but
after a little while she came over to him and
patted him.

A few months later they both made a visit
to Solbakken; Synnöve afterward came to visit
them: they over to Solbakken again and thus

it continued all the while they were growing up. Thorbjörn and Synnöve were rivals in their studies ; they went to the same school, and he became at last the more clever scholar of the two, — so clever that the priest interested himself in him. Ingrid did not get on so well; and both the others therefore helped her. She and Synnöve became so inseparable that people called them the " ptarmigans," because they always flew together, and both had very fair hair and complexions.

It happened, occasionally, that Synnöve got angry with Thorbjörn, because he was so excitable and fell into so many squabbles. Ingrid always acted as peacemaker, and then they became good friends again as before. But if Synnöve's mother heard of his fighting, he was not allowed to come to Solbakken that week, and hardly the next. No one dared tell Sæmund anything about such things ; " he is so severe with the lad," said his wife, and imposed silence upon all.

As they grew up, all three became good-looking, although each in his own way. Synnöve grew tall and slender, had flaxen hair, a finely moulded, bright face, with calm blue eyes When she spoke, she smiled, and people soon said it was a blessing to come within the atmos-

phere of her smiles. Ingrid was smaller, but
stouter, had still lighter hair, and a very little
face that was soft and round. Thorbjörn became of medium height, but was extremely well
formed, had dark hair, dark blue eyes, a sharply
cut face, and strong limbs. He had a habit of
saying of himself, when he was angry, that he
could read and write just as well as the school-
master, and feared no man in the valley, — except his father, he thought, but he did not add
that.

Thorbjörn wished to be confirmed early ; but
that could not be. " As long as you are not
confirmed you are only a boy, and I can better
control you ! " said his father. So it chanced
that he, Synnöve, and Ingrid went to the priest
at the same time. Synnöve, too, had waited un
usually long ; she was fifteen, in her sixteenth
year. " We never can know enough when we
come to make our confirmation vow," her
mother had always said ; and her father, Guttorm Solbakken, had answered " yes " to this.
So it was not strange that a couple of suitors
began to put in an appearance : one the son of
people of the better class, another a rich neighbor.

" It is too bad !   She is not yet confirmed ! "
" Well, then, we must have her confirmed.'

said the father. But Synnöve herself knew
nothing of this.

At the parsonage, the ladies of the priest's
family thought so well of Synnöve that they in-
vited her in, to talk with her. Ingrid and Thorbjörn waited outside among the rest, and when a
boy said to the latter, " So you did not get in
with her ? They are surely going to take her
away from you ! " it cost that boy a black eye.
From this time forth, it got to be a habit among
the other boys to tease him about Synnöve, and
it became apparent that nothing could throw
him into a greater rage. In a grove below the
parsonage there took place, at last, by agree-
ment, a big fight, which had this teasing for its
cause; the fight had grown to such an extent
that Thorbjörn had to deal with a whole crowd
at once. The girls had gone on in advance, so
there was no one to part them, and the fight
grew, therefore, worse and worse. He did not
want to give up; several attacked him at once,
and so he defended himself as best he could,
and the blows he dealt about him betrayed
afterwards what had taken place. The cause
came out at the same time, and it made a great
deal of talk in the parish.

The next Sunday there was service Thorbjörn would not go to church; and the next day

they were to go to the priest he feigned illness.
And so Ingrid went alone. He asked her, on
her return home, what Synnöve had said.

" Nothing."

When he joined the others again, he thought
that every one looked at him, and that the rest
of the class giggled. But Synnöve came later
than the others, and passed much time with the
priest's family that day. He feared a scolding
from the priest, but soon became aware that the
only two in the parish who knew nothing of the
fight were his own father and the priest. This
matter was not so bad, after all; but how he
should gain access to Synnöve again, he knew
not, for it was the first time that he did not
really like to ask Ingrid to intercede. After
the recitation was over, Synnöve was again in
at the priest's ; he waited as long as there was
any one else in the grounds, but at last he too
had to go. Ingrid had gone among the first.

The next day, Synnöve had come before all
the others, and was walking in the garden with
one of the young ladies and a young gentleman.
The young lady took up some flowering plants,
and gave them to Synnöve ; the gentleman as-
sisted ; and Thorbjörn stood among the rest
outside, and looked on. They explained to her
quite loud, so they all heard it, how these plants

were to be set out, and Synnöve promised to attend to them herself, that everything might be just as they said. "You cannot do it alone," said the gentleman, and Thorbjörn pondered over this. When Synnöve came out to the others, they showed far more respect for her than usual, but Synnöve went over to Ingrid, greeted her gently, and asked her to accompany her down to the green. There they seated themselves, for it was long since they had had a good talk together. Thorbjörn again was left with the others, and looked at Synnöve's pretty, strange flowers.

That day Synnöve went at the same time as the rest. "May I carry your flowers for you?" said Thorbjörn.

"Yes, if you like," she answered, kindly, but without looking at him, and taking Ingrid by the hand, went on ahead. At the foot of Solbakken she paused, and bade Ingrid farewell. "I can carry them myself the short distance that remains," said she, and took up the basket Thorbjörn had set down. The whole way he had been thinking about offering to plant the flowers for her, but now he could not muster the courage, for she turned away so abruptly. But afterwards he thought of nothing else except that he, still, ought to have helped her with those flowers.

" What were you two talking about ? " he
asked Ingrid.

" About nothing."

When the rest were well in bed, he quietly
dressed himself again and went out. It was a
beautiful evening, balmy and still ; the sky was
faintly overcast with bluish-gray clouds, here
and there torn asunder, so that it seemed as
though some one might be peering out from
the dark blue as from an eye. No one was to
be seen about the houses or farther away ; but
the grasshoppers were chirping all through
the grass, a rail piping on the right was answered on the left, and then there began a
singing in the grass from place to place, so that
it seemed to the wanderer as though he were
attended by a large company of followers, although he did not see a single one. The forest
stretched upwards, now blue, now dark and
still darker toward the rocky waste, and looked
like a great sea of mist. But through this he
heard the heath-cock strike up its note, a single
owl shriek, and the force chant its old, vigorous
rhymes louder than ever, now that all had set-
tled down to give ear thereto. Thorbjörn
looked over toward Solbakken, and went onward. He turned off from the usual path,
quickly reached the gard, and very soon stood

in the little garden that belonged to Synnöve, and that lay directly beneath the one loft window he knew so well, that of the chamber in which she slept. He listened and peered around, but all was still. Then he searched about the garden for working implements, and sure enough there he found both spade and hoe. The spading of a bed had been commenced; only a small corner was finished, but in it two plants were already set out, probably to see how they looked. "She became tired, poor girl, and left it," he thought. "It takes a man to do this," he thought further, and set to work. He did not feel the slightest desire for sleep; indeed, it even seemed to him that he had never performed so easy a task. He remembered how they were to be set out, remembered also the parsonage garden, and planted them accordingly. Night passed away, but he was not aware of it; he scarcely paused to rest, and had the whole bed spaded, the flowers set out, one here and there planted over again to give a better effect, and ever and anon he would steal a glance up at the chamber window to see whether any one was watching him. But neither there nor elsewhere was any one to be seen, nor did he hear so much as the barking of a dog before the cock began to crow, awaken ing the forest birds, who then, one after another, piped up their " good-morning " song. While he stood there patting down the earth around, the bed, he thought of the tales Aslak had told him, and how once he had believed that trolls and nisses grew over at Solbakken. He looked up at Synnöve's window, and smiled, as he wondered what she would think now in the morning hour. It had become pretty light, the birds were already making a terrible racket, and so he leaped over the fence and hastened home. No one should be able to say that it was he who had been there and set out flowers in Synnöve So.bakken's garden.

CHAPTER III.

Soon all kinds of things were said in the parish; but no one knew anything with certainty. Thorbjörn was not seen any more at Solbakken after he and Synnöve were confirmed, and this was what people could least understand. Ingrid often went over there; Synnöve and she would then usually take a walk in the wood. "Do not stay away too long!" the mother would call after them. "Oh, no," Synnöve would answer, and not come home before the dusk of the evening. The two suitors presented themselves anew. "She will have to attend to the matter herself," said the mother; the father thought the same. But when Synnöve was taken aside and questioned, they were rejected. Then several others made their appearance, but no one heard that they brought good luck home with them from Solbakken. Once, when her mother and she stood scouring some wooden milk-pans, the mother asked whom it was she was really thinking about. The question came so suddenly upon her that she blushed. "Have

you given any one a promise?" the mother
asked, and fixed her eyes on her. "No," answered Synnöve, promptly. There was nothing further said upon the subject.

As she was the best match in the parish,
she was followed by eager eyes when she appeared at church, the only place where she was
to be seen outside of her own home; that is
to say, she was never found at any dance or
other merry-making, because her parents were
Haugians. Thorbjörn sat directly opposite her
at church, but they never talked together, so
far as people could observe. Nevertheless, each
and every one felt assured that there must be
something between them; and as they did not
go about together in the same way as other
young lovers in the valley, there began to be a
great deal of talk. Thorbjörn did not seem to
be much liked. He probably felt this himself;
for he was pretty rough in his conduct when
several were together, as, for example, at dances
and weddings; and so it happened that now
and then he would rush into a fight. There
came a lull, however, after several had learned
how strong he was; and so Thorbjörn early
formed the habit not to brook having any one
stand the least in his way. "You are now re-
sponsible to yourself alone," said Sæmund, his

father; "but you will do well to remember that perhaps I am stronger than you."

Autumn and winter passed away; spring came, and still people knew nothing definite. There were circulated so many rumors concerning the refusals Synnöve had given that her company almost ceased to be sought. But Ingrid was her constant companion. They two were to go together to the sæter [1] this year, the Solbakken family having purchased a share in the Granlid sæter. Thorbjörn was heard singing up in the mountains, for he was getting ready one thing and another for them.

One beautiful day, when it was already drawing toward evening, and his work was done, he sat down to think matters over. His thoughts probably dwelt chiefly upon what was being talked of in the parish. He laid himself on his back in the red and brown heather, and with hands under his head he fell to gazing up at the sky, which moved so blue and glittering above the dense tree-tops. The green leaves and pine needles flowed out over it in a quivering stream, and the dark branches which cut through this made strange, wild designs therein. But the sky itself could only be seen when a leaf was wafted aside; farther away, through

---

[1] The mountain pasture.

the tree-tops, which did not touch one another,
it burst forth like a broad river, in whimsical
oscillations, and flowed over. This attuned his
mood, and he began to think of what he saw.

The birch laughed again, with its thousand
eyes, up at the spruce; the fir stood there with
silent contempt, its spikes bristling on every
side, for as the breeze gradually became more
caressing, more and more of the saplings quick-
ened, darted upward, and thrust their fresh foli-
age right under the nose of the fir. "Where
were you, I wonder, last winter?" inquired the
fir, waving to and fro, and perspiring rosin, in
an intolerable heat. "This is almost too bad !
— so far to the north. Whew ! "

But then there was an old, gray, bald fir, that,
towering above all the others, could still reach
down a many-fingered branch, almost perpendicularly, and seize a courageous linden by its
topmost poll, and make it shiver clear down to
its knees. This fathom-thick fir had had its
branches lopped by man, higher and higher up,
until at last, weary and disgusted, it suddenly
shot so far upward that the slender spruce at
its side became frightened, and asked whether
it, too, remembered winter's storms.

"Do I remember them?" said the fir, and
with the aid of the north wind boxed the

spruce's ears so smartly that it was not far from
losing its balance, and that was bad enough.
The large-limbed, dusky-hued fir had now
planted such a mighty foot in the ground that
its toes stuck out at least six yards off, and
were even thicker than the thickest part of the
willow, as the latter shyly whispered, one evening, to the love-sick hop-vine that twined itself up over it. The bearded fir was conscious
of its power, and said to man, as far beyond his
reach it put forth branch after branch, " Strip
me if you can ! "

" No, they cannot strip you ! " said the eagle,
as he graciously alighted on the fir, folded his
wings with dignity, and brushed some miserable
sheep's blood off his feathers. " I really think
I shall ask the queen to settle here; she has
some eggs she must lay," he added more softly,
and looked down at his bald legs ; for he was
ashamed because there came rushing over him
a quantity of tender memories of those earliest
spring days, during which one is apt to become
rather foolish with the first warmth of the sun.
Soon he raised his head again, and gazed from
beneath his feather-shaded brows up into the
dark mountain waste, in order to see whether
the queen, egg-laden and suffering, might not
be sailing about there. Off he then flew, and

the fir could soon see the pair far away toward
the clear, blue ether, where they were sailing
as high as the loftiest mountain peak, and were
discussing their household concerns. It cannot
be denied that the fir was a trifle anxious; for,
proud though it felt, it would be still prouder
to get a brace of young eagles to cradle. The
pair came down, and directly to it. They did
not speak to each other, but set right to work
to fetch twigs. The fir expanded, if possible,
more than ever; nor was there any one who
could hinder it from doing this.

But through the rest of the forest there was
a busy chatter, when it was seen what honor
had been bestowed on the great fir. Thus there
was a small, comely birch that stood mirroring
itself in a pond, and thought it had a right to
expect a little love from a gray wagtail that
was in the habit of taking a noonday nap on
its branches. It had buried the wagtail in fragrance clear up to its beak; it had covered
its leaves with insects, so that they were easy
enough to catch; nay, finally it had, in the heat,
built and bent together a well-sheltered little
house of twigs, thatched with fresh leaves, so
that the wagtail really was about to establish itself there for the summer. Now, however, the
eagle had taken up his abode in the great fir,

and off it must go. Here, indeed, was sorrow!
It trilled out a parting song, but very softly,
that the eagle might not notice it.

Some small sparrows, in the alder bush yonder, did not fare much better. They had kept
up such a clatter that a thrush, up in an ash
hard by, had never got to sleep at the right
time, had become furiously angry sometimes,
and had made a fuss. A solemn woodpecker
in the neighboring tree had laughed until it
had almost lost its footing. But then the eagle
was seen in the great fir! and the thrush and
the little sparrows and the woodpecker, and
every creature that had wings, must be off in
a great hurry, over and under the branches.
The thrush had sworn, as he flew away, that
he would never again take a house where he
had sparrows for neighbors.

So the whole forest stood there, forsaken, and
musing amidst the cheerful sunshine. It was
to have all its joy in the great fir, but that was
a poor joy. The forest bowed down anxiously
every time the north wind stirred, the great fir
beat the air with its mighty branches, and the
eagle flew in a circle around it, calm and com-
posed, as though this were merely a creeping
puff of wind, that was bearing upward some
paltry perfumes from the forest. But the whole

fir family was glad. Not one remembered that it would get no nest to rock this year.

"Away!" said the fir-trees; "we are of the same family."

"What are you lying tnere and thinking about?" asked Ingrid, who smilingly advanced from between some shrubs she was bending aside.

Thorbjörn started up.

"Oh, so many things can play in one's mind," said he, and gazed defiantly over the trees. "Besides, there is so much talk in the parish, in these days," he added, as he brushed some dust from his clothes.

"Why do you always trouble yourself so much about what people say?"

"Oh, I do not know, exactly; but — people have never yet said anything that was not in my mind, whether it was in my actions or not."

"That is a naughty thing to say."

"So it is," said he. Presently he added, "But it is true."

She sat down on the greensward; he stood with his eyes fixed on the ground.

"I can easily become what they want me to be; they had better let me be as I am."

"Then it really is your own fault, after all"

" That may be, but the rest have a share in it. I tell you, I want peace!" he almost shouted, and looked up at the eagle.

" Why, Thorbjörn!" whispered Ingrid.

He turned toward her, and laughed.

" Hush! hush!" said he. "As I told you, many things can play in one's mind. Have you spoken with Synnöve to-day?"

" Yes. She has already gone to the sæter."

" To-day?"

" Yes."

" With the Solbakken cattle?"

" Yes."

> " Tralala!
> The sun does his tree afar behold,
>   Triumlire!
> ' Art thou *there*, O thou, my own glittering gold?'
> Triumlit, triumling!
> Wakes the bird, with a spring.
> ' What is the matter?' "

" To-morrow we let loose *our* cattle," said Ingrid. She wanted to turn his thoughts in another direction.

" I am to go along and drive them!" said Thorbjörn.

" No, father wants to go himself."

" Ah, indeed!" observed he, and was silent.

" He asked for you to-day," said she.

" Did he?" said Thorbjörn, and cutting off a twig with his sheath knife, he began to strip the bark from it.

" **You** should talk more with father than you do," said she, gently. " He thinks a **great** deal of you," she added.

" That may be so," replied he.

" He often talks of you when you are out."

" All the less frequently when I am in."

" That is *your* fault."

"Perhaps it is."

" You must not talk so, Thorbjörn; you kncw very well what there is between you."

" What is there ? "

" Shall *I* repeat it ? "

" It may as well come out at once, **Ingrid** , you know as much as I do."

" Yes, to be sure. You will go your own way, and that you know he does not like."

" No; he would rather keep me in leading-strings."

" Yes, especially when you are going to fight."

" Are people to be allowed to do and say whatever they choose ? "

" No ; but you can keep out of their way. That is what father has done himself, and he has become a respected man by so doing."

" Perhaps he has been less tormented than I have been."

Ingrid was silent a little while; then she

continued, after glancing around her: "There is no use in speaking of this again; but still, whenever you know that enemies are in waiting, you ought to keep out of the way."

"No; that is just where I want to be! My name is not Thorbjörn Granliden for nothing."

He had stripped the bark from the twig; now he cut the latter in two. Ingrid fixed her eyes on him, and asked, rather slowly, "Are you going to Nordhoug on Sunday?"

"Yes."

After having sat silent for a while, without looking at him, she said again, "Do you know that Knud Nordhoug has come home to his sister's wedding?"

"Yes."

Now she looked at him. "Thorbjörn! Thorbjörn!"

"Shall he be allowed now any more than before to interfere between me and others?"

"He does not interfere, — not more than others wish."

"Nobody knows what others may wish."

"Yes, you do know well enough."

"At all events, she never says anything herself."

"Oh, how you do talk!" said Ingrid, looking displeased; and then, getting up, she glanced over her shoulder.

He flung away his bits of twig, put his knife into its sheath, and turned toward her.

" Listen ! I sometimes get tired of this. People ruin both my honor and hers with their gossip, for nothing is done openly. And, on the other hand, — I cannot so much as go over to Solbakken, — because her parents do not like me, she says. I am not allowed to visit her as other lads go to see their girls, because she is now one of the saints — to be sure ! "

" Thorbjörn ! " said Ingrid, becoming rather uneasy.

But he continued : " Father will not put in a word for me. ' If I deserve her I will get her,' he says. Stuff, nonsense, on the one side, and no compensation for it all on the other ! Why, I do not as much as know whether she really " —

Ingrid started forward, and placed her hand over his mouth, looking behind her as she did so. Just then the bushes were bent aside, and a tall, slender person, blushing rosy red, stepped forward : it was Synnöve.

" Good-evening ! " said she.

Ingrid looked at Thorbjörn as though she would say : " There, you can see for yourself ! " Thorbjörn glanced at Ingrid as though he wanted to say, " You should not have done so." Neither looked at Synnöve.

" I suppose I may be allowed to sit down a while ; I have walked so much to-day," and she seated herself.

Thorbjörn turned his head as if to see whether it was dry where she had sat down. Ingrid had let her eyes wander over to Granliden, and now she suddenly cried out, —

" Oh dear ! oh dear ! Fagerlin has got loose, and is going across the new-plowed field. The horrid beast ! What, Kelleros, too ? Well, that is really too much ; it is time for us to be off to the sæter ! " and she started down the slope, without even saying farewell. Synnöve arose at once.

" Are you going ? " asked Thorbjörn.

" Yes," said she ; but she stood still.

" You might as well wait a little," he observed, without looking at her.

" Another time," replied she, gently.

" That may be a long time hence."

She raised her eyes. He was looking at her too, now; but it was quite a while before either spoke.

" Sit down again," said he, a little embarrassed.

" No," she answered, and remained standing

He felt a sense of defiance rising within him; but just then she did something which he had not expected · she advanced a step, bent herself forward to him, looked up into his eyes, and said, with a smile, —

' Are you angry with me ? "

And when he ventured to return her look she began to cry.

" No!" replied he, his face flaming. He held out his hand; but as her eyes were full of tears, she did not see it, and he drew it back. Presently he said, " So you have heard it?"

" Yes," she answered, then looked up and smiled. But there were now more tears in her eyes than before. He knew not what he should do and say; therefore the words escaped his lips, —

" I have no doubt behaved too badly."

This was spoken very gently. She looked down and turned half away. " You should not judge what you know nothing about."

This was said in a half-choked voice, and it grieved him; he felt like a helpless boy, and so he said, as he could not think of anything else : " I beg your pardon."

But now she actually burst out crying. This he could not bear, but went over to her, put his arm about her waist, and, bending down

6

over her, said, "Do you really care for me
then, Synnöve?"

"Yes," she sobbed.

"But you are not happy?"

She did not answer.

"But you are not happy?" repeated he.

She now wept more than ever, and tried to
draw herself away.

"Synnöve!" said he, and tightened his hold.
She, still weeping, nestled up to him.   "Come,
we must talk a little together," continued he,
and he helped her to a seat in the heather; he
himself sat down by her side.   She dried her
eyes, and tried to smile; but she could not.
He took one of her hands, and looked into her
face.   " Dear, why cannot I come over to Solbakken?"

She was silent.

"Have you never urged this?"

She was silent.

"Why have you not done so?" he asked,
and now drew her hand nearer to him.

"I dare not," said she, quite softly.

His face grew dark; he moved one foot a
little toward him, and, resting his elbow on his
knee, laid his head in his hand.

"In this way, I shall probably never get over
there," said he, finally.

Instead of replying, she began to pull up the heather.

" Oh, yes, I have no doubt done many things which were not as they should be. But indeed, people might bear a little with me. I am not wicked " — he hesitated a moment ; "besides, I am still young, — only a little over twenty years old, but " — he could not finish the sentence at once. "But any one who is really fond of me," he added, " ought to " — and here he stopped outright. Then he heard, in suppressed tones at his side, —

"You must not talk so ; you do not know how much one — I dare not even tell Ingrid about it " — and again she burst into tears. " I — suffer — so — much ! "

He threw his arms around her, and drew her close to him. " Talk to your parents," whispered he, "and all will come right, you will see."

" It will be as *you* wish," she sobbed.

" As I wish ? "

Then Synnöve turned, and put her arm about his neck. " If you only cared for me as much as I do for you," said she, very lovingly, and with an attempt to smile.

" And do I not ? " asked he, softly and tenderly.

"No, no; you never take my advice. You know what will bring us together, but you never do it. Why do you not do it?" And as she now at length had begun to speak, her words flowed freely, and she continued in the same strain: "Ah me! if you only knew how I have longed for the day when I might see you over at Solbakken. But there is always something to hear which is not as it ought to be, and your own parents are the people who bring it over to us."

There was kindled, as it were, a light within him; and he now distinctly saw her moving about at Solbakken, waiting for a little peaceful moment when she might quietly speak of him to her parents; but he never gave her such a moment.

"You should have told me this before, Synnöve!"

"And have I not done so?"

"No, not as now."

She thought this over a little; presently she said, carefully laying small folds in her apron, "Then I suppose it was because — I did not quite dare."

But the idea of her being afraid of him touched him so deeply that, for the first time in his life, he gave her a kiss.

This so astonished her that she suddenly stopped crying; her eyes grew unsteady, as she tried to smile, looked down, then up at him, and now really smiled. They talked no more, but they found each other's hand again; neither ventured upon the slightest pressure. Then she drew gently back, began to wipe her eyes and her face, and to smooth her hair, as it had become somewhat disordered. He sat there thinking to himself, as he looked at her, "If she is more shy than the other girls in the parish, and wants to be treated in a different way, it will not do to make any objections."

He accompanied her up to the sæter, which lay not very far distant. He would have liked to walk hand in hand with her, but there had come something over him that made him scarcely dare touch her, and feel that it was strange that he was allowed to walk by her side.

When they parted, he said, "It shall be some time before you hear anything bad of me again."

At home, he found his father engaged in carrying grain from the store-house to the mill; for the people in tne parish round about had their grinding done at the Granlid mill, when the water in their own brooks had given out;

the Granlid mill-stream was never dry. There
were a great many bags to carry, some pretty
heavy, some exceedingly large. The women
stood near by, wringing the clothes they had
in the wash. Thorbjörn went over to his father, and laid hold of a bag. "Would you like
me to help you?"

"Oh, I can do it very well alone," said Sæmund, as he briskly lifted a bag on his back
and moved away toward the mill.

"There are many of them," said Thorbjörn;
and seizing two large ones, put his back up
against them, and drew them over his shoulders, each with one hand, while he steadied
them on either side with his elbow. Midway,
he met Sæmund, who was returning for more;
his father gave him a hasty glance, but said
nothing. As Thorbjörn, in his turn, went back
to the store-house, he met Sæmund with two
still larger bags. This time Thorbjörn took
a small one, and went with it; when Sæmund
met him he looked at him again, and longer
than the first time. So it happened that at
last they met at the store-house.

"There has come a message from Nordhoug,"
said Sæmund; "they want to have you at the
wedding on Sunday."

Ingrid looked imploringly over at him from
her work; his mother, too.

" Ah, indeed," answered Thorbjörn, dryly, but took this time the largest two bags he could find.

" Are you going ? " asked Sæmund, in a gloomy temper

" No."

CHAPTER IV.

THE Granlid sæter was beautifully situated, commanding a fine view of the parish; of Sol-bakken, first and foremost, with its many-hued groves about it, and then of the other gards, which lay forest-encircled, so that the green patch with houses in its midst looked like a peace-stead that had been discovered and forcibly snatched from the wild woodlands. There were fourteen gards that could be counted from the Granlid sæter; of the houses of the Granlid gard the roofs alone could be seen, and even these only from the extreme end of the sæter lawn. Nevertheless, the girls often sat watching the smoke which rose from the chimneys.

"Now, mother is cooking dinner," said Ingrid. "To-day they will have corned beef and bacon."

"Listen! they are calling the men," said Synnöve. "I wonder where they are working to-day," and the eyes of both girls followed the smoke that darted up in giddy haste through the clear, glad, sunny air, but soon slackened its speed, considered a while, then spread out in a broad processional sweep, growing ever thinner and thinner, until at last it became like a fluttering veil, and soon was scarcely visible. Many thoughts would then arise in their minds, and wander out over the parish. To-day the guests were all assembled at Nordhoug. It was a couple of days after the wedding, but as the festivities were to last six days, there reached them every now and then the report of a gun, and the voices of those who could shout the loudest.

" They are having a merry time there," remarked Ingrid.

" I do not envy them," said Synnöve, and took up her knitting.

" Still it would be interesting to be there," said Ingrid, who was sitting on her heels, and looking toward the gard, where the people were walking to and fro among the houses, — some going toward the store-house, where probably tables of refreshments were spread, others in pairs, separated from the rest, in confidential conversation.

" I do not quite know what there is to desire over there," said Synnöve.

" I scarcely know myself," replied Ingrid,

who sat as before. "I suppose it must be the dancing," she added.

Synnöve made no reply to this.

"Have you never danced?" asked Ingrid.

"No."

"Do you think, then, that dancing is a sin?"

"I really do not know."

Ingrid said nothing more upon the subject just then, for she remembered that the Haugians strictly forbade dancing, and she did not care to inquire further into the position Synnöve's parents took with her in this particular. But whatever train of thought she might have fallen into, she said, presently, "A better dancer than Thorbjörn I have never seen."

Synnöve paused a while before she said, "Yes, he is said to dance well."

"You should see him dance!" burst out Ingrid, turning toward her.

But Synnöve answered abruptly, "No, I do not wish to see that." Ingrid was a little surprised at this. Synnöve bent over her knitting, and began to count the stitches. Suddenly she let her knitting fall in her lap, gazed vacantly before her, and said, "So intensely happy, though, as I am to-day, I have not been for a long time."

"Why?" inquired Ingrid.

" Oh — because he is not dancing at Nord-houg to-day."

Ingrid sat lost in her own thoughts. " Well, there are, no doubt, many girls who would like to have him there," said she.

Synnöve parted her lips as though she were about to speak, but she did not utter a word, knit off the last stitch of a needle, and began on another.

" Thorbjörn probably longs to be there him-self ; I feel sure of that," said Ingrid ; but did not, until it was too late, consider what she had said, and looked at Synnöve, who sat there over her knitting, blushing crimson.

Now Ingrid was able to take a hasty review of the whole conversation ; she clasped her hands, moved on her knees over the heather until she brought herself in front of her, and began to look Synnöve squarely in the face ; but Synnöve went on knitting.

Then Ingrid laughed, and said, " Now, for many a long day you have been hiding some-thing from me, again."

" What do you say ? " asked Synnöve, and cast a questioning look at her.

" You are not angry because Thorbjörn dances," said Ingrid, laughing as before. The other did not answer. Ingrid's face was one broad smile, and now she put her arms about Synnöve's neck, and whispered in her ear, "But you are angry because he dances with others than you!"

"How you do talk!" said Synnöve, tore herself away, and arose. Ingrid got up also, and followed her.

"It is a pity that you cannot dance, Synnöve," said she, and laughed, — "really a great pity! Come, now, I might just as well teach you at once!"

She took Synnöve by the waist.

"What are you going to do?" inquired Synnöve.

"Teach you to dance, that you may not have such sorrow in the world as to have him dance with others than you!"

Now Synnöve too had to laugh, or at least make a show of laughing.

"Some one might see us," said she.

"Bless you for that answer, stupid as it was," replied Ingrid, and began forthwith to sing "tra-la-la," and move Synnöve round in step to it.

"No, no! It is not possible!"

"You have not been so happy for many a day, you said a while ago. Now, come!"

"If it only were possible!"

" Just try, and you will see that it is possible ! "

" You are so giddy, Ingrid ! "

" That is just what the cat said to the sparrow, when the sparrow would not stand still and let the cat catch him.   Come, now ! "

" Indeed, I actually feel inclined to, myself but " —

" Now I am Thorbjörn, and you are his young wife, who will not have him dance with any one but yourself."

" But" —

Ingrid sang again " tra-la-la."

" But " — Synnöve still insisted ; yet she was already dancing !   It was a spring-dance, and Ingrid went on in advance with great strides and manly swing of the arms ; Synnöve followed with short steps and downcast eyes, — and Ingrid sang : —

> " The fox once lay 'neath the birch-tree's root,
>   By the heather ;
> The hare came hopping there, on tripping foot,
>   O'er the heather.
> ' Well, this, indeed, is a sunny day,
>   And glitt'ring beams all around here play,
>   O'er the heather.
>
> " The fox then laughed in his quiet lair,
>   By the heather ;
> In wanton mood came frolicking the hare,
>   O'er the heather.

'I feel so glad over everything,
   Heigho ! — but you make a daring spring,
     O'er the heather.'

" The fox lay quietly waiting there,
   By the heather ;
And tumbling right toward him came the hare,
   O'er the heather.
' Good gracious ! why, is that you, my dear ?
Pray, how can you dare come dancing here
   O'er the heather ? ' " [1]

" There ! was it not possible ? " asked Ingrid as they paused, out of breath.

Synnöve laughed, and declared she would like better to waltz. " Why, there is nothing in the way of that," observed Ingrid, and they prepared for it at once by Ingrid showing her how she should place her feet ; " for waltzing is difficult," said she.

" Oh, it is easy enough, if we can only keep time," said Synnöve ; and so Ingrid suggested that they should try.

So they did, Ingrid singing and Synnöve joining in, at first only humming, then aloud. But suddenly Ingrid paused, let go of her, and clasped her hands in sheer astonishment. " Why, you can waltz ! " she broke out.

" Hush ! Do not let us talk about it any more," said Synnöve, and again took hold of Ingrid to continue.

[1] Auber Forestier's translation.

"But where did *you* learn " —

" Tra-la-la, tra-la-la ! " and Synnöve swung Ingrid round.

Then Ingrid danced to her heart's content, while singing, —

> "See, sunbeams dance on old Haukelid high;
> Dance, my sweetheart, for shades of evening draw nigh!
> The stream now leaps tow'rd the glitt'ring wave ;
> Leap, too, rollicking youth, leap on to thy grave!
> See, birch-trees bend to the wind's giddy play ;
> Bend, thou confident maid! What now did give way ?
> See " [1] —

What curious songs you are singing ! " said Synnöve, and stopped dancing.

" I do not know what I am singing; I have heard Thorbjörn sing them."

" They are Slave Bent's songs," said Synnöve. " I know them."

"Are they ? " asked Ingrid, and felt a little uneasy. She sat with her eyes fixed on the ground, and said nothing. All at once her attention was drawn to some one down on the road below. " Say, there is some one driving down from Granliden, and taking the parish road ! "

Synnöve looked that way, too. " Is it he ? ' asked she.

" Yes, it is Thorbjörn ; he is going to town.'

[1] Auber Forestier's translation.

It was Thorbjörn, and he was driving to town. It was a long distance off. He had a heavy load, and therefore drove leisurely along the dusty road. This was so situated that it could be seen from the sæter, and when he heard the shouting from above he knew who was there stood up on his load and shouted back again, so that it resounded through the mountains. Then the loor was played down to him; he sat and listened, and when it stopped he stood up again and shouted. This continued as he drove on, and it put him in high spirits. He looked at Solbakken, and thought it had never had so much sun as now. But while he sat there looking at it, he entirely forgot his driving, so that the horse went its own way. Suddenly he was startled by its making a great spring to one side, so that one thill cracked, and off went the horse in a wild trot across the Nordhoug fields; for it was over them the road lay. He stood up in the cart and drew in the reins. There arose a struggle between him and the horse; it was about dashing over a precipice, and he held it back. He got it so far that it reared, and then he sprang down, and before the horse could start on again he had caught hold of a tree; now the horse was forced to stand still. The load was overturned, one thill broken, and the horse stood and shivered. Thorbjörn went forward to the animal, took it by the bridle, and spoke gently to it; he at once turned it, to make sure of avoiding the precipice if it should start off again. Stand still it could not, so terrified was it, and he was compelled to follow it, running along, farther and farther on, straight up to the road again. He thus passed directly by his own things, which lay overturned; the pails and tubs broken, and their contents partly destroyed. Hitherto he had thought only of the danger; now he began to consider the consequences, and waxed wroth. It was plain to him that there would be no trip to town that day, and the more he reflected upon it the more vexed he became. Reaching the road, the horse gave another jump, then tried with one bound to tear itself loose; and now Thorbjörn's anger broke out. While he held the bridle with his left hand, with the great riding-whip in his right, he gave the horse lash after lash, lash after lash, on its flanks, until it was so maddened that it struck out at his breast with its fore-feet. But he held it off from him, and beat it now harder than before, with all his might, and using the butt end of his whip.

"I will teach you, you obstinate scamp!"

and he struck. The horse neighed and whinnied; he struck. " Ha! you shall make the acquaintance of a fist that is strong!" and he struck. The horse snorted until the foam rolled down over his hand; but he struck. " This shall be the first and last time, you cripple! There! Once more! So! Ho, you worthless nag, you shall learn how a man can punish!" and he struck.

Meanwhile, they had turned; the horse had ceased to offer any resistance, quivered and quaked under every blow, and crouched, neighing, whenever it saw the whip approaching. Then Thorbjörn became rather ashamed; he paused. At the same time he espied a man, who sat on the edge of a ditch by the roadside, leaning on his elbow, and laughing at him. He knew not how it happened; it grew dark before his eyes, and, holding the horse by one hand, he started toward the man with uplifted whip. " I will give you something to laugh at!" he shouted. The blow fell, but it half missed its mark, for with a shriek the man rolled down into the ditch. There he remained standing on all fours, but he raised his head, squinted at Thorbjörn, puckered up his mouth as for laughter; yet the sound of laughter was not heard. Thorbjörn was startled, for this face he had seen before. Yes, it was Aslak.

Thorbjörn did not know why, but there ran a cold shiver down his back. " I suppose it was you who frightened the horse both times," said he.

" Why, I was only lying there asleep," answered Aslak, and drew himself up a little; " and you woke me when you got so frantic over your horse."

" It was you who made the horse frantic. All animals are afraid of you," and he patted the horse, from whom the sweat was pouring in streams.

" I should think he would be more afraid of you now than of me. I have never acted so to any horse," said Aslak, who was now bolt-upright on his knees in the ditch.

" Do not use too strong language," said Thorbjörn, and shook his whip menacingly.

Aslak arose then, and scrambled up out of the ditch.

" I, you say, — I use strong language ? No ! "
" Where were *you* going, that you were driving so fast ? " said he, in a bland voice, as he approached Thorbjörn, but staggered from side to side, for he was drunk.

" I shall not have much chance of going beyond here to-day," said Thorbjörn, who was unhitching his horse.

"That is really provoking," said Aslak; and he drew still nearer, touching his hat as he did so. "Lord bless me!" said he. "Such a great fine fellow you have grown to be, since last I saw you!"

With both fists in his pockets, he stood, as well as he could, contemplating Thorbjörn, who could not get his horse loose from the wreck of the cart. Thorbjörn needed help, but he could not bring himself to ask it of this fellow; for Aslak looked ugly: his clothes were soiled from the ditch, his hair hung in matted tangles from under a glossy hat that was pretty old, and the face, although partly the well-known one of old, was now distorted into one continual broad grin, the eyes were still more closed than ever, so that he had to throw his head a little back and open his mouth a little, when he looked at any one. His features had become flabby, his whole form rigid; for Aslak drank. Thorbjörn had seen him frequently before, which Aslak did not let on that he knew. As a peddler, he had been in the habit of going the rounds of the parish, and was fond of being where there was any merry-making, as he had many songs to sing, told a good story, and got his brandy in return. Thus he had now been at the Nordhoug wedding, but had, as Thorbjörn afterwards learned, found it wise to absent himself for a time, as he had, according to an old trick of his, stirred the people up to a fight, and it threatened to break over his own head.

"You might just as well fasten him to the cart as try to get him loose from it," said he. "You will have to go up to Nordhoug, any way, to get things put in order again."

Thorbjörn had, no doubt, thought the same, but would have preferred not to think so. "There is a great wedding up there," said he.

"So much greater the help," replied Aslak.

Thorbjörn stood somewhat irresolute ; but without aid he could neither get forward nor backward, and so it was best to go up to the gard. He fastened his horse for the time, and started. Aslak followed. Thorbjörn looked back at him.

"So I go back to the wedding in good company," said Aslak, and laughed. Thorbjörn made no reply, but walked fast. Aslak came on behind, singing, —

"Two peasants once fared to the wedding feast," etc., —

an old, well-known ballad. "I say, you are walking fast," said he, presently. "You will get there, any way," he added.

Thorbjörn made no reply.

Sounds of dancing and music met them. Faces were visible peering out at them through the open windows in the great two-story building. Groups gathered together outside. He saw that they were querying among themselves as to who the new-comers could be; presently, that he was recognized, and that by degrees they descried the horse down yonder, and the pails and tubs which lay scattered over the ground. The dancing ceased; the whole crowd swarmed out into the gard just as Thorbjörn and Aslak came up.

"Here comes an unwilling wedding guest!" cried Aslak, as he finally approached the group, behind Thorbjörn.

The people greeted Thorbjörn, and speedily encircled him.

"God bless the gathering! Good ale on the table, pretty women on the floor, and good fiddlers on the stool!" cried Aslak, pushing himself, as he spoke, right into their midst.

Some laughed, others looked grave; one said, "Aslak, the peddler, is always in good spirits."

Thorbjörn at once found acquaintances, whom he had to tell about his accident; they would not allow him to go himself after his horse and things, but bade others go. The bride groom, a young man, and former school-mate, asked him in to taste of the wedding brewing; and now they passed on into the house. Some wanted to continue the dancing, especially the women; others wished to have a little time for drinking, and to get Aslak to tell them stories, since he had now returned to the gard again, in spite of everything.

" But you will have to be a little more on your guard than last time," one added.

Thorbjörn inquired where all the people were.

" Oh," was the reply, " there was a little disturbance here a while ago ; now some have gone to rest, others are over yonder in the barn, playing cards, and some are sitting where Knud Nordhoug is."

He did not ask where Knud Nordhoug was.

The bridegroom's father, an old man, who sat smoking a clay pipe and drinking ale, now said, " Come, out with a yarn, you Aslak ! It will be entertaining for once."

" Are there others who ask me ? " inquired Aslak, who had seated himself astride a stool, a little distance from the table, around which several others sat.

" Yes, to be sure," said the bridegroom, and gave him a dram ; " now I ask you."

"Are there many who ask in this way?"
said Aslak.

"It may be," said a young woman over on a
side bench, and offered him a stoup of wine.
It was the bride, a woman of about twenty
years of age, light complexioned, but very thin
and haggard, with large eyes, and rigid lines
about the mouth. "I like your stories very
well," she added.

The bridegroom looked at her, and his father
looked at him.

"Yes, Nordhoug folks have always liked my
yarns!" said Aslak. "Honor be to them!"
he exclaimed, and drained a glass which was
handed him by one of the groomsmen.

"Come, then, out with something!" shouted
several.

"About Sigrid, the gypsy woman," cried one.

"No, that is awful!" said others, especially
women.

"About the battle of Lier!" begged Svend,
the drummer.

"No; rather something amusing!" then said
a very erect lad, who stood in his shirt sleeves,
leaning up against the wall, while his right
hand, which hung relaxed at his side, rather too
frequently found its way into the hair of some
young girls who sat near him. They scolded,
but they did not stir.

" Yes, that is what I will tell, — yes, I will,"
said Aslak.

" The deuce ! " muttered an elderly man,
who lay across the bed smoking. One leg hung
down; with the other he kept kicking a fine
jacket, which hung over the bed-post.

" Let my jacket alone ! " called out the lad
who stood up against the wall.

" Let my daughters alone ! " rejoined he who
lay on the bed.

Now the girls moved away.

" Ho, I will tell what *I* please ! ' cried
Aslak. " For the brandy cup stirs the courage
up ! " said he, clapping together the palms of
his hands.

" Tell us what *we* please," reiterated the man
on the bed ; " for the brandy is ours."

" What does that signify ? " inquired Aslak,
with wide-opened eyes.

" Oh, the pig we fatten we kill, too," answered the man, dangling his leg.

Aslak closed his eyes, but sat still, without
changing the position of his head ; then it fell
on his breast, and he was silent. Several spoke
to him, but he did not hear them. " The
brandy has got the better of him," said he who
lay on the bed.

Presently, Aslak looked up, once more as

sumed his usual smile, and remarked, "Yes, now you shall hear a jovial tale. Lord bless me! how jovial!" said he, after a while, opening wide his mouth as though he were laughing, without any sound of laughter being heard.

"He is really in fine spirits to-day," said the bridgroom's father.

"Yes, indeed, he is!" cried Aslak. "A glass before starting, then!" said he, and stretched out his hand.

It was handed him. He drained it slowly, held his head a little back with the last drop in his mouth, then swallowed it, and, turning to him on the bed, said, "There, now, I am your pig!" and laughed as before. He clasped his hands about his knee, and thus raised his foot up and down, while he himself rocked to and fro, and then he began : —

"Well, once there was a girl who lived off in a valley. What the valley was called does not matter, nor what the girl's name was. But the girl was pretty; so thought the owner of the gard at — hist! — and it was at his place she served. She received good wages, she did, and she got more than she should have had, — she got a child. Folks said that it was by him; but he did not say so, for he was married, nor did she say so, for she was proud, the poor wretch.

So there was, no doubt, a lie told at the christ-
ening ; and the child she had brought into the
world was an outcast of a boy, so that it really
did not matter if he was christened in a lie. A
tenant house down below the gard was given
to her, which the wife at the gard did not like,
as might have been expected. Whenever the
girl came up there she spit after her, and when
the little lad of hers came to play with the
gard-boys she told them to drive the bastard
away ; he deserved nothing better, she said.

"The wife begged her husband, both by
night and by day, to turn the wretched girl on
the parish. The man resisted so long as there
was anything of a man left in him ; but at last
he fell to drinking, and then his wife got the
upper hand. After that the poor wretch had a
hard time of it ; every year it grew worse, and
got so at last that she was on the verge of starv-
ing to death, with her little boy, who would not
go away from his mother.

"So it continued, year after year, until eight
of them had passed by ; still the girl had not
left the place, although now she was forced to
go away. And so she went. But first the
entire gard was in a fine blaze, and the man
ourned to death, for he was drunk. The wife
saved herself and the children, and she said it

was that miserable girl down at the tenant
house who had kindled the fire. It might be
that this was so. And it might also be otherwise. That was a singular boy of hers. For
eight years he had seen his mother roughing
it, and knew well where the fault lay, for she
had often told him when he asked why she was
always crying. She had done so the day before she was to leave, and that was why *he* had
gone off at night. But *she* was imprisoned for
life, because she told the judge herself that it
was she who had made the fine blaze up at the
gard. The boy lived on the parish, and got
help from everybody, because he had such a
wicked mother. Then he left this parish, and
went far away to another, where he did not
receive much aid, for there he found no one
who knew what a wicked mother he had. I
do not think he told of it himself. The last I
heard of him he was drunk, and they say he
has given himself up to drink of late : whether
this be true or not shall remain unsaid ; but it
is true that I do not know what better he could
do. He is a bad, wicked fellow, that is certain ;
he does not love people, loves them still less
when they are good to one another, and least
of all when they are good to him. And he
wants others to be like himself, although he

says so only when he is drunk. And then he cries, too, cries so that it hails, about nothing in the world ; for what should he have to cry about ? He has not stolen a shilling from any one, nor done a single one of the wild things many others do; so he really has nothing to cry about. Nevertheless, he does cry, and cries so that it hails. And if you should see him cry never believe in it, for it is only when he is drunk, and then he is not to be noticed."

Here Aslak fell back on the stool in a loud fit of weeping, which was soon over, for he dropped asleep.

"Now the swine is drunk," said the man on the bed; "that is the way he always lies blubbering in his sleep."

"That was horrid," said the women, and arose to go away.

"I have never heard him tell anything different when he was allowed to choose for himself," now said an old man, over by the door, getting up. "The Lord knows why folks will listen to him," he added, looking at the bride.

CHAPTER V.

SOME went out; others tried to get the fiddler to come in again, that the dancing might begin; but the fiddler was asleep in a corner of the passage, and a few begged for him that he might be left in peace. "Since Lars, his comrade," they said, "was hurt in the fight, Ole had been obliged to hold out over twenty-four hours."

The men had arrived at the gard with Thorbjörn's horse and things; his horse was hitched to another cart, since, in spite of all urging, he would insist on going again. It was the bridegroom, in especial, who tried to detain him. "There may, perhaps, not be as much happiness for me here as it would seem," said he; and this suggested a thought to Thorbjörn; but he nevertheless resolved to leave before evening came. When they saw that he was firm, they scattered over the grounds; there were many people present, but there was an oppressive stillness, and, indeed, little appearance of a wedding. Thorbjörn needed a new

harness-pin, and went off to find one ; at the
gard there was no suitable material, and so he
went a little outside, and came to a wood-shed,
which he entered slowly and quietly, for the
words of the bridegroom haunted him. He
found what he wanted, but furthermore, without being conscious of what he was doing, he
seated himself against the one wall, with a
knife and the pin in his hand. Then he heard
a groaning near by ; it was on the other side
of the thin wall, in the carriage-house, and
Thorbjörn listened.

" Is that — really — you ? " he heard, uttered
with a long interval between the words, and by
a man who spoke with difficulty. Then he
heard some one weeping, but that was not a
man.

" Oh, why did you come here ? " was asked ;
and it must have been by the one who was
weeping, for the voice choked with tears.

" Hm ! At whose wedding should I play, if
it was not at yours ? " said the first.

" It must be Lars, the fiddler, who lies there,"
thought Thorbjörn. Lars was a strong, handsome fellow, whose old mother was tenant of a
houseman's place, belonging to the gard. But
the other must be the bride.

" Why have you **never** spoken ? " said she, in

a smothered voice, but slowly, as though deeply moved.

"I did not think it was necessary, between us two," was his short answer.

There was silence for a while; then she began again: "You knew, though, that *he* came to see me."

"I thought you were stronger."

He heard nothing now but weeping; finally, she burst out once more, "Why did you not speak?"

"It would have been of little use for old Birthe's son to speak to the daughter of Nordhoug," was answered, after a pause, during which he drew his breath heavily, and often groaned. A reply was waited for.

"We have had our eyes on each other for many a year," came at last.

"You were so proud, I did not exactly dare speak to you. Yet there was nothing in the world I desired more. I expected every day — when we met — I thought the next time I would offer myself. Then I thought you slighted me."

All was still again. Thorbjörn heard no reply, no weeping; nor did he even hear the sick man's breathing.

Thorbjörn thought of the bridegroom, whom

he believed to be a worthy man, and he felt troubled for him. Then she, too, said, "I am afraid he will have little happiness in me, — he, who" —

"He is a good man," said the sick one, and began to break down again, for his chest, no doubt, pained him.

It seemed as though this gave her pain, too, for she said, "It is pretty hard for you now — but — we would most likely never have chanced to talk together, had not this thing happened. When you struck Knud, I understood you for the first time."

"I could bear it no longer," said he; and then, presently, "Knud is base."

"He is not good," said Knud's sister.

They were silent for a while; then he said, "I wonder if I shall ever get over this. Ah, well, though, it is all one now."

"If you have a hard time, it is worse for me," and hereupon followed convulsive weeping.

"Are you going?" asked he.

"Yes," was the reply; and then, "Ah, woe, woe is me! What a life this will be!"

"Do not cry so!' said he. "The Lord will soon put an end to it for me, and then **you** shall see that it will be better for you, too."

8

"Alas, alas, if you had only spoken!" she cried, in a suppressed voice, and as though she were wringing her hands.

Thorbjörn thought she must either have gone away at the same time, or at least be unable to talk longer; for he heard nothing for a while, and went away.

Of the first person he met in the gard Thorbjörn asked, "What has happened between Lars, the fiddler, and Knud Nordhoug?"

"Ha! Between them? Well," said Per, the houseman, wrinkling his face as though he wanted to hide something in the folds, "you may well ask, for it was little enough : Knud only inquired of Lars whether his fiddle gave out good tones at this wedding."

Just then the bride went past them. She had her face averted, but when she heard Lars mentioned she turned it, and showed them a pair of large red eyes, which were unsteady in their gaze; otherwise her countenance was very cold, so cold that Thorbjörn did not recognize her words again in it. He began then to understand more.

Farther on in the gard the horse stood waiting. Thorbjörn fastened in his pin, and looked around for the bridegroom, in order to take his leave. He did not feel like searching for him soon saw that he was not coming, and took his seat upon the cart. Then there was heard the sound of noisy talking and shouting on the left side of the gard, over in the direction of the barn. There was a great crowd pouring out of the barn; a large man, who walked on in advance, was crying, " Where is he? Is he hiding? Where is he?"

" There, there!" said some.

" Do not let him come here," said others; " only mischief will arise from it."

" Is that Knud?" inquired Thorbjörn of a little boy who stood at the side of his cart.

" Yes; he is drunk, and when he is he always wants to fight."

Thorbjörn was already seated on his load, and now he whipped up his horse.

" No, stop, comrade!" he heard behind him. He reined in his horse, but as it started off in spite of this, he let it go. " Ho! Are you afraid, Thorbjörn Granliden?" was shouted nearer him. Now he reined in still more firmly, but did not look back.

" Get down now, and come into good company!" some one cried.

Thorbjörn turned his head. " Thank you, I must go home," said he.

Now they consulted together a little, and im-

mediately the whole crowd flocked to the cart.
Knud went forward to the horse; he first
patted it, then took it by the head to look at
it. Knud was very tall; had light but straight
hair, and a snub nose; the mouth was large
and heavy; his eyes were light blue, but bold.
He bore little resemblance to his sister; yet
there was something about the mouth which
was similar, and he had the same kind of square
forehead, but smaller, although all her fine
features were coarse with him.

"What will you take for your nag?" asked
Knud.

"I do not want to sell it," said Thorbjörn.

"You think, perhaps, I cannot pay for it,"
said Knud.

"I do not know whether you can or not."

"So? You doubt it? You had better take
care," said Knud.

The lad who had stood against the wall in
the house fingering the hair of those girls now
said to a neighbor, "Knud really does not dare
this time."

This Knud heard. "I dare not? Who says
so? I dare not?" he shrieked.

More and more came flocking up. "Make
way! See the horse!" shouted Thorbjörn, and
cracked his whip; he wanted to start.

"Are you saying 'make way' to me?" asked
Knud.

"I spoke to the horse; I must go on," said
Thorbjörn, but did not turn aside himself,
either.

"What! will you drive right over me?"
asked Knud.

"Then move away!" and the horse had to
throw back his head, else it would have sent it
right against Knud's breast. Then Knud took
the horse by the bridle, and the animal that
remembered being held so on the road, began
to tremble. This, however, touched Thorbjörn,
who repented what he had done to the horse;
now he vented his feelings on Knud; for he
started up with the whip in his hand, and gave
Knud a blow on the head.

"Do you strike?" shrieked Knud, and came
nearer. Thorbjörn sprang from the load.

"You are a villain!" said he, pale as death,
and threw the reins to the lad from the house,
as he had come forward and offered his services.

But the old man who had risen from his
seat over by the door, when Aslak was through
with his story, now approached Thorbjörn, and
pulled him by the arm. "Sæmund Granliden
is too good a man to have his son fight with
such a bully," said he.

This quieted Thorbjörn down, but Knud shouted, " I a bully? That he is as well as I, and my father is just as good as his! Come on! It is absurd that the parish folks do not know which of us two is the champion," he added, and pulled off his neck-tie.

" We will test that soon enough," said Thorbjörn.

Then the man who had been lying on the bed before said, " They are like two cats ; they have to growl courage into each other, both of them."

Thorbjörn heard this, but made no reply. One and another of the crowd laughed ; others said it was abominable to have all these fights at this wedding, and to pick a quarrel with a stranger, who wanted to go away peaceably. Thorbjörn looked around for his horse ; it was his intention to drive off. But the lad who had taken charge of it had turned it round, and led it away quite a distance ; the lad himself stood just behind them.

" What are you looking for ? " asked Knud. " Synnöve is a long way off now."

" What is she to you ? "

" Nothing. Such hypocritical women-folks are nothing to me," said Knud. " But perhaps it is she who has stolen your courage away."

This was too much for Thorbjörn ; they noticed that he glanced around, to make sure of the lay of the ground. Now some of the older people interfered, and remarked that Knud had done mischief enough for this wedding.

" He shall do me none ! " said Thorbjörn and when they heard this they were silent.

Others said, " Let them wrestle, and then they will be good friends ; these two have long enough been throwing spiteful glances at each other."

" Yes," said one, " they both want to be first in the parish ; let us see how it is."

" Have you people seen anything of a certain Thorbjörn Granliden about here ? " remarked Knud. " I thought he was at the gard, just now."

" Yes, here he is," said Thorbjörn, and at the same time he gave Knud a blow on the right ear that sent him reeling against some men who stood there. Now all was still. Knud got up again, and darted forward, without saying a word. Thorbjörn was ready for him. There now followed a long hand-to-hand fight, each trying to get at the other ; but both were well accustomed to hold off an opponent. Thorbjörn's blows fell rather oftener, and some said were somewhat more severe.

" There, Knud has found his man," said he
who had taken the horse.   Make way ! "

The women fled ; only one stood high up on
a step, in order to see better ; it was the bride.
Thorbjörn caught a glimpse of her, and hesitated a little ; then he saw a knife in Knud's
hand, remembered her saying that Knud was
not good, and with a well-aimed blow he hit
Knud's arm on the wrist, making the knife
drop, and paralyzing the arm.

" Oh, how you hit ! " said Knud.

" Do you think so ? " said the other, and now
rushed at him.

Knud was at a disadvantage, having the use
of only one arm, he was lifted up and borne on,
but he made resistance before he was pros-
trated.   He was several times thrown to the
ground, with such force that any one else
would have yielded, but his was a good back.
Thorbjörn moved on with Knud; the people
gave way, but Thorbjörn kept coming on with
him ; and thus it continued around the entire
gard, until they came to the steps, where Thorbjörn tossed Knud once more into the air, and
flung him down with such violence that his
knees gave way, and Knud fell across the stone
slab, so that it sang within him.   He lay there
without stirring, gave vent to a deep groan

and closed his eyes; Thorbjörn straightened himself, and looked up; his eyes fell directly on the bride, who stood motionless, and looked on. "Take something and lay it under his head," said she, turned, and went in.

Two old women went by; one of them said to the other, "Good God! there lies some one again! Who is it now?"

A man answered, "It is Knud Nordhoug."

Then the older woman said, "Well, perhaps there will be less of fighting after this. They might have some other use to put their strength to."

"That was a true word you said, Randi," said the first. "The Lord help them on so far that they can look beyond one another, and up to something *better*."

This had a curious effect on Thorbjörn's mind; he had not uttered a word, but still stood motionless, watching those who were busied with Knud. Several spoke to him, but he made no reply. He turned away from them, and fell into a reverie; Synnöve was uppermost in it, and he became much ashamed. He wondered what explanation he should give her, and he thought that it was, after all, not so easy for him to stop fighting as he had be-ieved. Just then, he heard some one behind

him say, " Beware, Thorbjörn ! " but before ne
could turn, he was seized by the shoulders from
behind, was bent down, and felt nothing but a
burning pain, the locality of which he did not
precisely know.   He heard voices about him ;
was conscious that some one was driving; even
thought, at times, that he was driving himself,
but was not sure of it.

This lasted a very long time.   It grew cold,
soon warm again, and then he felt so light, so
light, that he seemed to be floating.   And now
he understood it : he was borne on the tree-
tops, from one to the other, and thus went up
the slope ; higher up, as far as the sæter ; still
higher up, as far as the highest mountain.
There Synnöve bowed over him, and wept, and
said that he should have spoken.   She wept
sorely, and said that he must have seen, himself, how Knud Nordhoug got in his way, continually in his way, and so she was obliged to
take Knud.   And then she stroked him gently
down one side, so that it grew warm there, and
she wept until his clothes became wet in the
place where her tears fell.   But Aslak sat on
his heels upon a great peaked stone, and set
fire to the tree-tops round about him, so that
they crackled and burned, and the twigs drifted
about him ; then he laughed, with wide gaping

mouth, and said, " It is not I, it is my mother,
who is doing this ! " And Sæmund, his father,
stood a little to one side, and tossed up bags of
grain so high that the clouds drew them up to
themselves, and spread out the grain like a
mist; and it seemed strange to him that the
grain could float out over the whole sky. When
he looked over at Sæmund himself, the latter
had grown so small, so very small, that at last
he scarcely reached above the ground ; but still
he went on tossing the bags up higher and
higher, and said, " Do *that* like me, if you
can ! " Far away, in the clouds, was the church,
and the fair woman from Solbakken stood up
in the steeple, waving an orange-colored handkerchief in one hand and a hymn-book in the
other, and said, " Hither you shall not come,
until you have laid aside fighting and swearing." And when he came to look there, it was
not the church, but Solbakken, and the sun
shone so brightly on all the hundred window-
panes that it hurt his eyes, and he had to close
them tight.

" Take care, take care, Sæmund ! " he heard
and was awakened as though from slumber by
being carried onward · and when he looked
about him he had come into the family-room
at Granliden. A great fire was burning on

the hearth; his mother stood beside him and
wept; his father just then put his hands under
him; he wanted to carry him into a side room.
Then his father laid him gently down again.
" There is still life in him!" said he, with a
quivering voice, and turned to the mother.

She burst out, " The Lord help me! he is
looking up! Thorbjörn, Thorbjörn! My
blessed boy, what have they done to you?"
and she bent over him and stroked his cheek,
while her warm tears fell on his face.

Sæmund wiped his eyes with one arm, then
drew the mother tenderly aside. " I might just
as well take him at once," said he; and he took
firm hold under the shoulders with one hand,
and a little farther down the back with the
other. " You hold his head, mother, if he has
not strength to carry it himself." She walked
on before and supported his head; Sæmund
tried to keep step with her, and soon Thorbjörn lay on the bed in the other room. After
they had covered him and placed him just right,
Sæmund asked whether the boy had started.

" There he is!" said the mother, and pointed
toward the window.

Sæmund opened the window, and called out,
" If you are there in an hour you shall have
your year's wages doubled! It does not matter if you break the horse's wind."

He went over to the bed again. Thorbjörn fixed on him his large clear eyes; the father was forced to return the gaze, and then his own grew moist. "I knew it would end so," said he softly, turned and went out.

The mother sat on a stool at the foot of the bed and wept, but she did not speak. Thorbjörn wanted to talk, but he felt that it was difficult, and therefore he was silent. But he stared incessantly at his mother, and she had never seen such lustre in his eyes, nor had they ever been so beautiful, which seemed to her a bad omen. "May the Lord help you!" she burst out, at last. "I know that Sæmund will break down completely the day you leave us." Thorbjörn looked at her with immovable eyes and face. That look went right through her, and she began to say the Lord's Prayer for him; for she thought his time might be short. While she sat there it ran through her mind how dear he, beyond the others, had been to them all; and now none of his brothers and sisters were at home. She sent word up to the sæter for Ingrid and a younger brother; then came back and seated herself as before. He still looked at her, and that look was to her a psalm, which gently guided her thoughts to better things; and old Ingebjörg grew very devout,

brought forth the Bible, and said, " Now I will
read aloud to you, and it will do you good."
And as she had no spectacles at hand she opened
at a place that she had nearly known by heart
since she was a girl, and this was in the Gospel
of John. She was not sure that he heard her ;
for he lay motionless as before, merely staring
at her ; but still she read on, if not for him, at
least for herself.

Ingrid soon came home to relieve her in the
watch ; but then Thorbjörn was asleep. Ingrid
wept without ceasing ; she had commenced crying before she left the sæter, for she thought of
Synnöve, to whom nothing had been told. Now
the doctor came and examined him. He had
been stabbed with a knife in the side, had been
beaten besides ; but the doctor said nothing, and
there was no one who questioned him. Sæmund went with him into the sick-room, stood
there watching uninterruptedly the doctor's face,
went out when he went, helped him up in his
cariole, and touched his cap when the doctor
said he would come again the following day.
Then Sæmund turned to his wife, who had accompanied him : " When that man does not
speak, it is alarming." His mouth quivered ;
he turned on his heel, and went away across
the field.

No one knew what became of him; for he did not come home that evening, nor in the night either, but appeared first the next morning; and then he seemed so gloomy that no one dared ask him anything. He said himself, " Well ? "

" He has slept," said Ingrid, " but he is so weak that he cannot raise a hand."

The father wanted to go in and look at him, but he turned when he came to the door.

The doctor was there, and he came the next day, and several days in succession. Thorbjörn could speak, but was not allowed to stir. Ingrid sat most of the time with him; also his mother and younger brother ; but he did not ask them about anything, nor they him. The father was never in there. This they saw the patient noticed ; every time the door opened he grew attentive, and they thought it must be because he was expecting his father. At last Ingrid asked if he would not like to see others of the family. " Oh, they most likely do not want to see me," replied he. This was told to Sæmund, who made no immediate reply ; but that day he was away when the doctor came. When the doctor had proceeded a piece along the road, he saw Sæmund, who sat by the wayside waiting for him. After having greeted him, Sæmund inquired about his son.

"He has been roughly handled," was the short reply.

"Will he get over it?" asked Sæmund, and fell to adjusting the horse's saddle-girth.

"Thank you, that is all right," said the doctor.

"It was not tight enough," replied Sæmund.

There was a brief silence, in which the doctor looked at him; but Sæmund was zealously tightening the girth, and did not look up.

"You asked whether he would get over it; yes, I think he will," said the doctor, slowly.

Sæmund glanced up, hastily. "Is there hope of life?" asked he.

"There has been for several days," replied the doctor.

Then a few tears trickled down from Sæmund's eyes; he strove to brush them away, but they came again. "It is really a shame that I am so fond of the lad," he gasped; "but you see, doctor, a finer fellow there has never been in the parish!"

The doctor was touched. "Why have you not wished to know anything before?" he asked.

"I have not had the courage to hear it," replied Sæmund, and had another struggle with his tears, which he could not force back.

" And then there were the women-folks," he
continued; " they were constantly on the look-
out to see whether I would ask, and then I
could not." The doctor gave him time to com
pose himself, and then Sæmund looked fixedly
at him. " Will he get his health back again? "
asked he, suddenly.

" In a certain way, although we cannot yet
be sure of it."

Then Sæmund grew calm and thoughtful.
" In a certain way," he muttered. He stood
looking down, and the doctor would not disturb
him, because there was something about the
man which forbade it. Suddenly Sæmund
raised his head. " Thank you for the information," said he, held out his hand, and started
for home.

Meanwhile, Ingrid was sitting with the patient. " If you feel able to listen, I will tell
you something about father," said she.

" Tell me," replied Thorbjörn.

" Well, then, the first evening the doctor had
been here father disappeared, and no one knew
where he was. Now it seems that he had gone
over to the wedding-party, and all the people
there felt ill at ease when he came in. They
say that he sat down among them and drank
with them, and the bridegroom tells that he

9

thinks he grew half tipsy. Then first he began
to question about the fight, and got the full
particulars as to how it had happened. Knud
came in; father wanted to have *him* tell all
about it, and made him go with him out to the
spot where you two wrestled. All the people
went with them. Knud then told how you had
treated him after you had lamed his hand; but
when Knud did not want to say anything more,
father drew himself up, and asked if this was
the way it went on *afterward*, — and at the
same time he seized Knud about the chest,
raised him, and laid him down on the stone,
which still had your blood on it. He held him
down with his left hand, and drew out his knife
with the right. Knud changed color, and all
the guests were silent. There were people
there who saw father shed tears, but he did
nothing to Knud. Knud himself did not stir.
Father then lifted Knud up, but laid him down
again after a while. 'It is hard to let you go,'
he said, and stood staring at him, while he still
held him.

"Two old women went past, and one of them
said, 'Think of your children, Sæmund Granliden!' They say that father at once let go of
Knud, and that pretty soon after he was gone
from the gard; but Knud left the wedding

made his way on from house to house, and was seen there no more."

Scarcely was Ingrid through with her narration when the door opened; some one looked in, and it was the father. She went out at once, and Sæmund came in. What father and son then talked about no one ever knew; the mother, who stood up against the door that she might listen, thought once that she heard them speaking about whether Thorbjörn could recover his health or not. But she was not sure of it, nor did she like to go in as long as Sæmund was there.

When Sæmund came out he was very gentle, and rather red about the eyes. "He will be spared to us," he said to Ingebjörg, as he passed by; "but the Lord only knows whether he will get his health back again." Ingebjörg began to cry, and went out with her husband; on the store-house steps they sat down, side by side, and many things were talked over between the two.

But when Ingrid came softly in again to Thorbjörn, he lay there with a little note in one hand, and said calmly and slowly, "This you may give to Synnöve the next time you see ner."

When Ingrid had read what was in it she

turned away and wept; for the note ran
thus : —

"*To the highly esteemed maiden, Synnöve, Guttorm's
daughter, Solbakken : —*

"When you have read these lines, all must
be over between us two. For I am not the one
you ought to have. The Lord be with us both.
    "THORBJÖRN, SÆMUND'S SON, GRANLIDEN."

CHAPTER VI.

SYNNÓVE had learned of the disaster the day after Thorbjörn had been at the wedding. His younger brother had been sent up to the sæter with word about it; but Ingrid had detained him out in the passage, just as he was starting, and had charged him with what he was to say. Synnöve, therefore, only knew that Thorbjörn had overturned his load, and that he therefore had been obliged to go up to Nordhoug for help; that Knud and he had met, and that Thorbjörn had been somewhat hurt. He was in bed, but it was nothing dangerous. This was news calculated to make Synnöve more vexed than alarmed. And the more she thought about it, the more disheartened she became. Whatever he might promise, he was sure to act so that her parents would have some fault to find with him. But they two ought not to be separated now, any way, thought Synnöve.

There were not many messages sent up to the sæter, and so time dragged before Synnöve got further news. The uncertainty weighed heavily upon her mind, and as Ingrid did not come back again, there must be something amiss. She was not able to sing the cattle home in the evening, as she had been in the habit of doing, and she did not sleep well at night, for she missed Ingrid. The effect of this was that she felt weary by day, and this did not make her heart any lighter. She went about her daily duties, scoured the wooden pans and bowls, made the cheese, and prepared the curds, but took little satisfaction in it; and both Thorbjörn's younger brother and the lad who tended the herds with him felt sure now that there must be something between her and Thorbjörn, which furnished them with a theme for many conversations up in the pasture.

The afternoon of the eighth day after Ingrid had been summoned home she felt more oppressed than ever. So long a time had now passed away, and still no tidings. She left her work to sit down and gaze over the parish, for this seemed to her a sort of company, and she did not want to be alone now. As she sat there, she grew very tired, laid her head down on her arm, and directly fell asleep; but the sun scorched, and it was a restless sleep. She was over at Solbakken, up in the loft, where her things were, and where she used to sleep

from the flowers in the garden there was wafte?
up a most delicious fragrance, although no
that which she was accustomed to, but something different, almost like that of heather.
" What can this come from ? " she thought, and
bowed her head down out of the open window.
Yes, truly, there stood Thorbjörn, down in the
garden, planting heather. " Why, my dear,
what are you doing ? " asked she. " Oh, the
flowers will not grow," replied he, and went on
working in the garden. This made her sorry
for the flowers, and she finally begged him to
bring them up to her. " Yes, I will, if you
wish," said he, and then he gathered them up,
and came toward the house with them. But
she did not seem to be in the loft any more, for
he could come right in to where she was. At
that moment her mother appeared. " Good gracious ! Is that horrid Granlid boy coming in
here to you ? " cried the mother, as she sprang
forward, and stationed herself directly in his
way. But he insisted upon coming in, not-
withstanding this; and now a struggle arose
between the two. " Mother, mother ! he is
only bringing my flowers back to me ! " said
Synnöve, beseechingly, and wept. " Oh, that
makes no difference," said the mother, and continued to struggle. And Synnöve was fright-

ened, terribly frightened, for she knew not
which of them she wanted to win ; but neither
of them must lose. "Be careful of my flowers ! " cried she. But they struggled now
harder than ever, and the pretty flowers were
strewn around everywhere; the mother trod
upon them, and so did Thorbjörn. Synnöve
wept. But when Thorbjörn had dropped the
flowers, he looked so ugly, so very ugly; his
hair grew, his face, too ; his eyes had a wicked
look, and he stuck long claws into her mother.
"Take care, mother! Do you not see that it is
some one else, — take care ! " she shrieked, and
made a move to go over and help her mother,
but she could not stir from the spot. Then
some one called her, and called a second time.
Immediately Thorbjörn disappeared, the mother
also. Then some one cried again.

"Yes ! " said Synnöve, and awakened.

"Synnöve ! " the voice called.

"Yes ! " answered she, and looked up.

"Where are you ? " was asked.

"It is mother who is calling," thought Synnöve, as she rose, and went back toward the
sæter lawn, where the mother stood, with a
lunch box in one hand, and shading her eyes
with the other, looking toward her.

"You were actually lying there asleep on
the bare ground ! " said the mother.

" I grew so sleepy," replied Synnove, " that
I just lay down for a little while, and before I
knew it I was asleep."

" You must be careful not to let such things
happen, my child. Here is something for you
in this box; I baked yesterday, as father is
going on a long journey."

But Synnöve felt clearly that her mother
had not come for this, and she thought that
she had not been dreaming of her for nothing.
Karen (that was the mother's name) was, as has
been said before, small of stature and slender,
had fair hair, and blue eyes that were constantly
in motion. She smiled a little when she spoke,
but it was only when she talked with strangers.
Her face had grown rather sharp. She was
quick in her movements, and was always busy.
Synnöve thanked her for her gift, took off the
lid, and looked to see what was in the box.

" There, there you can do *that* another time,"
said the mother. " I noticed that your bowls
had not been washed yet; you must see to
that, my child, *before* you take your rest."

" Yes; but that has only happened to-day."

" Come, then, I must help you, since I am
here," said the mother, and rolled up her skirts.
" You must accustom yourself to order, whether
you are under my eyes or not."

She moved on to the dairy, and Synnöve followed slowly. They took every article out and washed it. The mother then inspected all the work, and found that it was not bad; gave much advice and helped to clean up; and thus an hour or two passed. While they were working she told what was going on at home, and how busy she was now and would be until she got father off. Then she asked if Synnöve remembered to read the word of God before she went to bed at night. "For you must not forget that," she observed, "or else the work will fare badly the next day."

As soon as they were through, they went out on the lawn, and sat down there to wait for the cows. And when they were well seated the mother inquired after Ingrid, and asked if she was not soon coming up to the dairy again. Synnöve knew no more about this than her mother. "Aye, to think that folks should act so!" said the mother; and Synnöve clearly understood that it was not Ingrid she meant. She would have liked to change the subject, but had not the courage to do so. "They who never have our Lord in their hearts are found out by Him sometimes when they are least expecting it," continued the mother. Synnöve spoke not a word. "Well, this I have alway said: the boy will never amount to anything. But to act so — it is a shame!" They were sitting side side by there, and gazing out over the landscape beyond; but they did not look at each other. "Have you heard how he is getting on?" asked the mother, and now glanced hastily at her.

"No," answered Synnöve.

"They say he is in a bad way," said the mother.

Synnöve's heart grew faint. "Is it, then, serious?" asked she.

"Oh, he was stabbed with a knife in the side; and then he had some pretty severe blows, besides."

Synnöve felt that she was blushing crimson; at once she turned a little more away, so that her mother could not see her. "Well, it is not a very serious matter, I presume?" said she, as calmly as she could.

But her mother had observed that her breast heaved violently, and so she answered, "Oh, no. I cannot say that, either."

Now Synnöve began to suspect that something dreadful had happened. "Is he in bed?" she asked.

"Why, bless me! of course he is in bed! It is a pity for his parents, such worthy people as they are. He has been well brought up, too, so that the Lord has nothing to blame them for." Synnöve was now so anxious that she knew not what she should do. Presently her mother continued, " Now it proves to be well that no one is bound to him. The Lord has done everything here also for the best." Synnöve grew very dizzy, and it seemed as though she would glide down the side of the mountain. " Well, I always said to father, God have mercy on us ! said I. We have only this one daughter, and we must take care of her. Now he is rather inclined to be too yielding, excellent man as he otherwise is ; therefore it is a good thing that he takes counsel where he finds it, and that is in the word of God."

But at the mere thought of her father, and how gentle he always was, Synnöve had still more difficulty in forcing down the tears, and this time no resistance was of any avail ; she began to weep.

" Are you crying ? " asked her mother, and looked at her, without being able to see her face.

" Yes ; I was thinking of father, and then ' — and she burst out crying, in good earnest.

" But, my dear child, what is the matter ? "

" Oh, I do not really know ! It came over

me — perhaps some harm will come to him on this journey," sobbed Synnöve.

" How you do talk! " said the mother. " All should not go well with him? Going to town on a smooth country road? "

" Yes, but remember — what happened — to the other," faltered Synnöve.

" To him? Yes! But your father does not go dashing ahead like a fool-hardy simpleton, I should think. *He* will come home again unharmed, — provided the Lord will watch over and guide him."

The mother began to get an idea from the weeping, which now it seemed impossible to stop. Presently, without moving from her place, she said, "There are many things in the world which are hard to bear, but we must take consolation in knowing that they might be far worse."

" Aye, but that is poor consolation," said Synnöve, and wept sorely.

The mother did not really have the heart to answer what she thought; she merely said, " The Lord himself ordains many things for us in a plainly visible way · He has doubtless done so in this case also." And then she arose, for the cows were beginning to come lowing up the ridge, the bells tinkled, the herd-boys shouted, and they came down slowly, for the cows were well filled and quiet. She stood and looked on; then bade Synnöve come with her and see to the cows. Synnöve now arose, too, and followed her, but they went slowly.

Karen Solbakken busied herself with welcoming the cattle. The cows came up one by one, and they knew her and lowed; she patted them, talked to them, and felt happy when she saw how they had all improved.

"Ah, yes," said she, "the Lord is near to *those* who keep themselves near to Him."

She now helped Synnöve to put them in; for Synnöve made slow progress to-day. The mother did not comment on this. She helped her also to milk, although by so doing she remained up there longer than she had intended. When they had finished straining the milk, the mother began to prepare to go home, and Synnöve wanted to go with her part of the way.

"Oh, no," said her mother, "you are doubt-'ess tired, and would like to be left in peace." And she took the empty box, held out her hand, and said, looking fixedly at her, "I will come up again soon to see how things are going with you. Cling to us, and do not think of others."

Scarcely was the mother out of sight before

she began to consider how she could most quickly get a message down to Granlid. She called Thorbjörn's brother. She wanted to send him down, but when he came she found that it would be embarrassing to confide in him, and so she said, "It was nothing." She then thought about going herself. Certainty she must have, and it was a pity Ingrid had sent her no word. The night was quite light, and the gard was not so far off but that she could easily walk that distance, when such a matter as this drew her down there. While she sat thinking of this, she summed up in her thoughts all that her mother had said, and began to weep afresh. But this time she was not slow; she threw a kerchief about her, and took a roundabout way, so that she might escape the notice of the boys.

The farther she advanced, the more she hastened, and at last she sprang down the foot-path, so that the small stones were loosened, rolled down, and frightened her. Although she knew it was only the stones rolling, she thought there must be some one near by, and she was compelled to stand still and listen. It was nothing, and she hurried on faster than before. Then it chanced that she came down with a bound on a large stone, whose one end protruded into the road, but which now gave way, dashed on and past her. It made a terrible racket, the bushes crackled, and she was afraid, but grew still more so when she really fancied that there was some one who rose and moved farther on down the road. First she thought that it might be a wild beast. She paused, and held her breath ; down below on the road, what she had seen also paused.

"Hoy!" cried a voice. It was her mother. The first thing Synnöve did was to hasten away and hide. She kept still a good while, in order to find out whether her mother had recognized her, and was coming back; but she went on. Then she waited still longer, in order that her mother might get well out of the way. When she started on again, she walked slowly, and was soon approaching the houses.

When she saw these, she began to grow oppressed again, and she grew more faint the nearer she came to Thorbjörn's home. All was still there. The implements of labor stood leaning up against the wall ; the wood was chopped and piled up, and the axe stuck fast in the block. She walked past these, and on to the door ; there she paused, looked around, and listened ; but nothing stirred. As

she stood there, uncertain whether she should
go up-stairs to Ingrid or not, it came into her
mind that it must have been on such a night,
some years ago, that Thorbjörn had been over
and planted her flowers. Swiftly she pulled
off her shoes, and stole up the stairs.

Ingrid was much frightened when she woke
up, and saw that it was Synnöve who had
awakened her. " How is he getting on? "
whispered Synnöve. Now Ingrid recalled everything, and she wanted to begin to dress, in order to avoid answering Synnöve immediately.
But Synnöve seated herself on the edge of the
bed, begged her to lie still, and repeated her
question.

" He is better now," said Ingrid, in a whisper. " I am soon coming up to the sæter."

" Dear Ingrid, hide nothing from me ; you
can tell me nothing so bad that I have not fancied something worse."

Ingrid still tried to spare her, but Synnöve's
alarm increased, and there was no opportunity for evasive answers. In a whisper were
dropped the questions, in a whisper the answers ; the deep silence round about heightened
the seriousness of both questions and answers,
so that it grew to be one of those solemn mo-
ments in which people dare to look the worst

10

truth directly in the face.   But this much they
both seemed to decide upon, that Thorbjörn's
fault was small this time, and that nothing
bad on his side intruded itself between him
and their sympathy for him.   They both wept
freely, but quietly, and Synnöve wept the most;
she sat quite crushed on the edge of the bed.
Ingrid tried to cheer her by reminding her of
how much happiness they three had had together ; but, as is so often the case, every little
remembrance from those days over which sunshine played, now in their sorrow melted into
tears.

"Has he asked after me?" whispered Synnöve.

"He has scarcely spoken at all." Ingrid
now thought of the note, and it began to weigh
upon her.

"Is he, then, not able to talk?"

"I do not know how it is with him; he
probably thinks the more."

"Does he read?"

"Mother has read to him; now she has to
do so every day."

"What does he say then?"

"Oh, he says almost nothing, as I told you
He only lies there and looks."

"It is in the painted chamber he lies?"

"Yes."

"And turns his head toward the window?"

"Yes."

They both were silent for a moment; then Ingrid said, "The little St. John's toy you once gave him hangs in the window, and keeps turning round."

"Yes, it is the same," said Synnöve, suddenly and firmly. "Never in the world shall any one get me to give him up, whichever way it may turn!"

Ingrid felt greatly distressed. "The doctor does not know whether he will recover his health," she whispered.

Now Synnöve stopped crying, raised her head, looked at her without saying a word, then let it fall again, and sat still, lost in thought; the last tears trickled slowly down her cheeks, but no new ones followed them. She clasped her hands, but otherwise did not stir; it was as though she sat there forming a great resolve. She then suddenly arose, with a smile, stooped down over Ingrid, and gave her a warm, long kiss. "If he becomes an invalid, then I will take care of him. Now I will speak with my parents." This touched Ingrid deeply; but before she could find words she felt her hand grasped. "Farewell, Ingrid! Now I will go up alone." And she turned away, hastily.

" There was that note," whispered Ingrid
after her.

" That note ? " questioned Synnöve.

Ingrid was already up, had found it, and went
over to her with it; but as with her left hand
she thrust it into Synnöve's bosom, she put her
right about her neck and kissed her, while Synnöve felt her great, warm tears fall on her face.
Then Ingrid softly pushed her out of the door,
and closed it; for she had not the courage to
see any more.

Synnöve went slowly down the stairs, in her
stocking feet; but when her thoughts became
too much for her, she inadvertently made a
noise, grew alarmed, hurried out of the passage, seized her shoes, and, with them in her
hand, hastened away past the houses, across
the fields, and over to the gate.   Here she
paused, put them on, began to go up the path,
and made haste, for her blood coursed rapidly
through her veins.   She walked on, singing
softly to herself, and hurried more and more,
so that at last she grew weary, and had to sit
down.   Then she remembered the note.

When the shepherd dogs began to make a
noise the next morning, the herd-boys had
awakened, and the cows were to be milked and
set free, Synnöve had not yet returned.

As the boys stood wondering where she could be, and discovered that she had not been in bed the whole night, Synnöve appeared. She was very pale and quiet. Without a word, she began getting breakfast for the herd-boys, put up their lunches, and afterwards helped to milk.

The fog still hung heavily over the low ridges; the heather glittered with dew all over the sorrel-tinted heights. It was rather chilly, and when the dog barked he was answered on every side. The cattle were set free; lowing they greeted the fresh morning air, and the cows, one by one, started off over the foot-path; but there in front of them sat the dog, ready to receive them and hinder them from passing until every one had been let loose, whereupon he also let them go. The bells vibrated along the ridge; the dog barked, making the welkin ring; the herd-boys tried which of them could shout the loudest. From all this noise Synnöve moved away down to that part of the sæter where Ingrid and she were in the habit of sitting. She did not weep, sat there quietly with her eyes fixed before her, and gave heed now and then to the tumultuous noise which was gradually becoming more distant, and which blended the better the farther away it got. Meanwhile, she began to hum softly to herself, then to

sing louder, and at last with a clear, high
voice, the following song. She had adapted it
from another one she had known from the
time she was a child: —

"Now thanks for all since we two were small,
    In groves we played, at each merry-making;
I thought our sports would float onward all
    'Till Time's gray twilight was breaking.

"I thought our sports from the birch would rise,
    Leaf-crowned and glad, and would upward wander
To where bright Solbakken meets the eyes,
    The old red church seeking yonder.

"Of evenings oft I did sit and wait,
    The spruce-grown forest there watching ever;
The mountains darkened, the hour grew late,
    But thou, ah thou, camest never!

"I sat and waited, and oft I thought:
    When day declines he will venture over;
But fading light flick'ring flashes brought,
    The days they came and passed over.

"The weary eye is accustomed now
    To seek one way, 't would be slow at changing;
It burns and aches here beneath the brow,
    Yet still one way it is ranging.

" At Fagerlid, in the church, they say,
    I 'll comfort find, as is surely fitting;
But ask me not to go there, I pray,
    For he, by my side, there is sitting.

"And yet so well who it was, I know,
    Who placed our homes there so near together,
And cut a way for the eye to go
    Through woods, o'er flowery heather.

" And yet so well who it was, I know,
  Who placed the seats at the Lord's own table,
And caused that people in pairs to go
  Toward the chancel are able." [1]

[1] Auber Forestier's translation.

CHAPTER VII.

SOME time after this, Guttorm Solbakken and Karen sat together over in the great, light sitting-room at Solbakken, and read aloud to each other from some new books they had procured from the neighboring town. They had been at church in the forenoon, for it was Sunday; then they had taken a little walk together through the grounds to examine the condition of the fields, and to consider which land should be allowed to lie fallow and which should be plowed up for the next year. They had sauntered from one pasture and field to another, and it seemed to them that the gard had improved greatly in their time. "God knows how it will prosper when we are gone!" Karen had remarked. Then it was that Guttorm had begged her to come in with him that they might read in the new books; "for one does best to avoid such thoughts."

But now the books had been examined, and Karen was of opinion that the old ones were better. "People only write over again what is in the old books," said she.

" There may be something in that. Sæmund
said to me to-day in church that children were
only their parents over again."

" Yes, you and Sæmund evidently talked of
many things to-day."

" Sæmund is a sensible man."

" But he seeks his Lord and Saviour too little, I am afraid."

To this Guttorm made no reply.

" What became of Synnöve ? " asked the
mother.

" She is up-stairs," answered Guttorm.

" You were sitting there with her yourself,
a while ago; what frame of mind was she in ? "

" Oh " —

" You should not have allowed her to stay
there alone."

" Some one came in."

The wife was silent for a while. " Pray,
who was it ? "

" Ingrid Granliden."

" I thought she was still at the sæter."

" She was at home to-day in order that her
mother might be able to go to church."

" Yes, to be sure, we saw her there for once."

" She has a great deal to do."

Others have the same; nevertheless, one
generally manages to go where one longs to
be."

Guttorm made no reply to this.

After a while Karen said, " All the Granlid family were there to-day except Ingrid."

" Yes, it was probably to accompany Thorbjörn the first time."

" He looked poorly."

" No better could be expected. I only wonder he appeared so well."

" Yes, he has had to suffer for his folly."

Guttorm looked down a little, as he replied, " He is only in his youth yet."

" There is no good foundation there; one can never feel sure of him."

Guttorm, who sat with his elbows on the table, twirling a book round with one hand, now opened it, and just as though he were reading softly dropped the sentence, " He is said to be quite sure of fully regaining his health."

The mother now took up a book also. " That is, indeed, a good thing for such a fine-looking lad," said she. " May the Lord teach him to use it better ! "

They both read; but presently Guttorm said, as he turned over a leaf, " He did not look toward her once during the whole day."

" Yes, and I noticed, too, that he kept his seat in the pew until she had gone out."

After a while, Guttorm asked, " You think he will forget her ? "

" That would at all events be best."

Guttorm read on; the wife turned over the leaves. " I do not care much to have Ingrid stay here," said she.

" Synnöve has scarcely any one else to talk with."

" She has us."

Now the father glanced over at her. " We must not be too strict."

The wife was silent. Soon she said, " Nor have I ever forbidden her to visit with Ingrid."

The father closed his book, arose, and looked out of the window. " There goes Ingrid," said he.

Scarcely had the mother heard this than she hastily left the room. The father remained for some time at the window; then turned and walked up and down. The wife came in again, and he paused.

" Yes, it was as I thought," said she. " Synnöve is sitting up there crying, but rummages about in her trunk when I come in." And then she added, shaking her head, " No, it is not well to have Ingrid coming here ; " and she betook herself to preparing the evening meal, passing often in and out.

Once while she was out Synnöve came in, rather flushed from weeping and quiet; she walked close by her father, into whose face she looked up as she passed, and over to the table, where she sat down and took a book. Presently, she closed this, and asked her mother if she should help her.

"Yes, do so!" said the latter. "Work is good for all things."

It became her task to set the table; it stood over by the window. The father, who thus far had been walking to and fro, went over there now and looked out. "I believe that barley field the rain beat down is straightening up again," said he. Synnöve took her stand by his side, and looked out, too. He turned; his wife was in, and so he merely stroked the back of Synnöve's head with one hand, after which he began pacing the floor again.

They ate their supper, but very quietly. The mother said grace that day both before and after the meal, and when they had arisen she desired them to read and sing, which they did, too. "The word of God gives peace; it is after all the greatest blessing in a house." With this the mother looked over at Synnöve, who had cast down her eyes. "Now I am going to tell you a story," said the mother; "it is true, every word, and not bad for those who will reflect upon it."

And then she began as follows : " There was, in my younger days, a young girl at Houg, who was the granddaughter of a learned old lens-mand. He early took her under his own care, that he might have joy in her in his old days, and of course taught her the word of God and good behavior. She was quick at learning and delighted in knowledge, so that in the course of time she was far in advance, while we stood behind ; she wrote and ciphered, knew all her school-books and twenty-five chapters in the Bi-ble, when she was fifteen years old. I remem-ber it as though it were yesterday. She cared more for reading than for dancing, so that she rarely was to be found at the merry-makings, but oftener in her grandfather's loft-chamber, where he kept his many books. It so hap-pened that whenever we did meet her she always seemed to be somewhere else, and we said to one another, ' Were we only as wise as Karen Hougen ! ' She was to inherit the old man's property, and many a good fellow offered himself to share it with her ; but they all got refusals. About this time the priest's son came home from the priest-school. Things had not gone well with him, because he had more taste for carousing and mischief than for proper things ; now he drank. ' Beware of him ! ' said

the old lensmand. 'I have been much with people of the upper classes, and it is my experience
that they are less worthy of our confidence than
peasants.' Karen constantly heeded his voice
beyond that of others. And when, by and by,
she began to come into contact with the priest's
son she avoided him, for he sought her. Soon
she could go nowhere without meeting him.
'Away!' cried she; 'it will do you no good.'
But he persisted, and thus it happened that at
last she was forced to pause and listen. He
was handsome enough, but when he told her
that he could not live without her he frightened
her. He was always hanging about the house,
but she did not come out; he stood outside of
her window at night, but she did not appear;
he said he would put an end to himself, but
Karen knew what she knew. And then he
would take to drinking again. 'Beware of him!
These are all the devil's snares,' said the old
lensmand. One day the fellow appeared in her
room; no one knew how he had come there.
Now I am going to kill you,' said he. 'Yes,
lo so if you dare,' said she. But then he shed
tears, and told her that it was in her power to
make a respectable man of him. 'If you could
abstain from drinking even half a year,' said
she. And so he kept from drinking half a

year. ' Do you trust me now? ' asked he. ' Not until you have given up all kinds of gayety and merry-making for half a year.' This he did. ' Do you trust me now? ' asked he. ' Not until you go away and finish your studies for the priesthood.' He did this, too, and the next year came back with his studies completed. ' Do you trust me now? ' asked he, and even had on gown and collar. ' Now I should like to hear you preach a few times,' said Karen. And he preached strictly in accordance with the word of God, as it behooves a priest to do ; he spoke of his own weakness, and how easy it was to conquer if one could only begin, and how good the word of God was when once it was found. After this he again sought Karen. ' Yes, now I believe you live up to what you have learned,' said Karen. ' And now I will tell you that for three years I have been betrothed to my cousin, Anders Hougen; you shall publish the bans for us next Sunday.' "

Here the mother concluded. Synnöve had paid little attention in the beginning, but had gradually roused up more and more, and at the last hung upon every word. " Is there any more? " inquired she, much alarmed.

" No," answered the mother. The father looked at the mother, and then her gaze grew

unsteady and avoided his ; and after a little re-
flection, during which she drew her finger along
the table, she continued, " Perhaps there might
be something more ; but it does not matter."

" Is there more ? " asked Synnöve, turning
to her father, who seemed to know about it.

" Oh — yes ; but it is as mother says ; it does
not matter."

" What became of him ? " asked Synnöve.

" Ay, that is just it," said the father, and
looked toward the mother. She had leaned
back against the wall, and was looking at the
two.

" Did he become unhappy?" asked Synnöve,
softly.

" We must end where the end ought to be,"
said the mother, and arose. The father did
likewise. Synnöve slowly arose after them.

CHAPTER VIII.

SOME weeks later, early in the morning, the entire Solbakke household was preparing for church-going. There was to be confirmation, which took place a little earlier this year than usual, and on an occasion of this kind the house was always locked up, for all wanted to go. They were not going to drive, as the weather was clear, although rather cold and blustering in the morning; the day promised to be fine. The road wound about the parish; and past Granliden, then took an abrupt turn to the right, and fully two miles farther on lay the church. The grain was in most places cut and put on poles for drying. The cows had nearly all been brought down from the mountains, and were tethered. The fields were either covered with their second growth of green, or where the earth was poor were of a grayish-white hue. Round about stood the many-colored forests: the birch already drooping, the aspen quite yellow, the rowan with dry, shriveled leaves, but with berries. It had rained

hard for several days; the small brush that
lined the roadside, and stood sneezing in the
sand, was now washed clean and fresh. But
the mountain sides began to beetle more darkly
over the valley, now that the devastating autumn had dismantled them and made them
look sober; whereas the mountain brooks,
which had only occasionally shown life during
the summer, rolled swollen and leaped down
with a great noise. The Granlid force fell
more heavily and with more gravity, especially
when it came to the rocky waste of the Granlid
slope, where the mountain suddenly refuses to
accompany it any farther, and makes an abrupt curve inward. It braced itself in the rock,
and then rushed onward, and shouted so that
the mountain trembled. The rock was well
washed for its treason, for the force sent a provoking jet of spray right up into its face.
Some inquisitive alder bushes, which had approached the edge of the precipice, had nearly
reeled down in the flood; they stood gasping
in the shower-bath, for the force was not spar-
ing to-day.

Thorbjörn, both his parents, his brother and
sister, and the rest of the household passed by
and beheld this. He was now well again, and
had already taken vigorous hold of his father's

work, as before. The two were continually together, and so they were to-day.

"I almost think those are the Solbakke people we have right behind us," said the father.

Thorbjörn did not look back, but the mother said, "Yes, so they are; but I do not see — oh, yes, far back there."

Either because the Granlid family went faster after this, or because the Solbakke family slackened their speed, the distance between them became greater and greater; at last they could scarcely see one another.

It looked as if the church would be crowded; the long parish road was black with people, walking, driving, and riding. The horses, now in the autumn, were full of mettle and little accustomed to being together; the result of which was that they went neighing along, and were so unruly that the trip was dangerous, although quite lively. The nearer they drew to the church, the greater noise the horses kept up; for each one that arrived called out to those who already stood tied there, and they in turn tugged at their tethers, stamped on the ground with their hind hoofs, and whinnied at the new-comers. All the dogs of the parish, who the whole week long had sat listening to one another, scolding and teasing one another,

now met here at church, and rushed into the
most desperate fights, in couples and in great
knots, all over the grounds. The people stood
quiet in rows along the church wall and along
the houses, spoke in whispers, and merely
looked at one another out of the corners of
their eyes. The road leading past the wall was
not broad; the houses on the opposite side
were close by; and the women generally stood
along the church wall, the men directly opposite, along the houses. Not until later did they
venture to cross over and mingle together; and
even if acquaintances espied one another at a
distance they acted as though they did not
know one another until that time came. It
might then happen that when a fresh party
came up some of those already there stood so
directly in their way that a greeting could not
be avoided; but it was given, in such cases,
with half-averted face and few words, whereupon the new-comers were apt to withdraw
each to his side. When the Granlid family
approached, the prevailing stillness, if possible, increased. Sæmund did not have many
to greet, and so he quickly passed down the
line; the women, on their part, at once fastened themselves against the wall, and remained
standing there among the foremost. The re-

sult of this was that when it was time to go
into church the men had to cross over again
after the women. Just as they were doing so,
three vehicles, one after the other, came driving up more rapidly than any of the preced-
ing ones, and did not slacken their speed as
they turned in among the people. Sæmund
and Thorbjörn, who came near being run over,
both looked up at once ; in the first vehicle sat
Knud Nordhoug and an old man, in the second his sister and her husband, and in the third
his parents. Father and son looked at each
other ; not a feature of Sæmund's face moved.
Thorbjörn was very pale. They both gazed
away and looked directly before them; then
they saw the Solbakke family, who had just
paused directly opposite to greet Ingebjörg and
Ingrid Granliden. The vehicles had come in
between ; conversation had grown stiff ; their
eyes still hung on those who had driven on,
and it was some time before they could withdraw them. After one and the other had begun to recover from the surprise, and let their
eyes wander around to seek something to di-
vert their attention, they fell on Sæmund and
Thorbjörn, who stood staring there in the road.
Guttorm Solbakken turned away, but his wife
at once sought Thorbjörn's eyes. Synnöve,

who had probably caught these, turned to Ingrid Granliden, and took her hand to greet her,
although she had done so once before. But
they all at the same time became conscious that
their servants and acquaintances were every one
observing them, and Sæmund went right over
and, without looking at him, took Guttorm by
the hand.

"Thanks for last," [1] said he.

"Thanks to yourself for last."

To Guttorm's wife too he said, "Thanks for
last."

"Thanks to yourself for last;" but she did
not look up as she spoke.

Thorbjörn followed, and did as his father had
done. The latter had now come to Synnöve, who
was the first person he looked at. She looked
up at him, too, and forgot to say, "Thanks for
last." Thorbjörn appeared just then; he said
nothing, she nothing. They took each other by
the hand, but lightly; neither could raise an
eye, neither could stir a foot.

"It is surely going to be blessed weather, to-
day," remarked Karen Solbakken, and glanced
hastily from one to the other.

It was Sæmund who answered: "Oh, yes;
that wind is driving the clouds away."

---

[1] A common greeting in Norway, equivalent to "Thanks for the
last time we were together."

"That is a good thing for the grain that is standing out and needs dry weather," said Ingebjörg Granliden, and began to brush the back of Sæmund's jacket, probably because she thought it was dusty.

"The Lord has given us a good year; but it is rather uncertain whether we shall get everything under cover," began Karen Solbakken, and glanced over again at the two, who had not stirred since the last time she looked.

"That depends upon how strong a force we can muster," replied Sæmund, and turned in such a way toward her that she could not very well look where she wanted. "I have often thought that a couple of gards might unite their forces; we would surely do better in that way."

"It might happen that they would want to make use of the dry weather at the same time," said Karen Solbakken, and took a step to one side.

"Yes, to be sure," answered Ingebjörg, and stationed herself close beside her husband, so that Karen could not look where she desired now either. "But in some places the crop ripens earlier than in others; Solbakken is often a fortnight in advance of us."

"Yes, and so we could very well help each

other," observed Guttorm slowly, and drew a step nearer. Karen gave him a hasty glance. "However, there are many circumstances which can come in the way," added he.

"That there are," said Karen, and moved a step to one side, a step to the other, and still another, but glanced back again.

"Oh, yes, there is often a great deal in one's way," said Sæmund; and a smile seemed to play about his lips.

"That is no doubt so," said Guttorm.

But his wife interposed, "Man's power does not extend far; that of God is the greatest, I should think, and it depends upon Him."

"Do you think He is likely to have anything especial against our helping one another with the harvesting at Granliden and Solbakken?"

"No," remarked Guttorm. "He cannot have anything against that," and he looked gravely at his wife. She turned the subject.

"There are a great many people at church to-day," said she; "it does one good to see them seek the house of God."

No one seemed to want to reply; finally Guttorm observed, "I really believe the fear of God is increasing; there is a larger attendance at church now than there was in my young days."

"Oh, yes, — the people are increasing," remarked Sæmund.

"No doubt there are some among them, perhaps the greater part, who merely come over here from habit," said Karen Solbakken.

"Perhaps the younger ones," observed Ingebjörg.

"The younger ones like to meet one another," said Sæmund.

"Have you heard that the priest is going to apply for another parish?" asked Karen, thus turning the conversation a second time.

"That would be too bad," said Ingebjörg. "He has both baptized and confirmed all my children."

"I suppose you would like him to marry them also, first," said Sæmund, and chewed away at a chip he had picked up.

"I wonder if it will not soon be church time!" exclaimed Karen, and looked over at the door.

"Yes, it is pretty warm out here to-day," said Sæmund, chewing away as before.

"Come now, Synnöve, let us go in."

Synnöve started, and turned, for she had doubtless been talking with Thorbjörn.

"Will you not wait until the bell rings?" asked Ingrid Granliden, and stole a glance at Synnöve.

"Then we can all go in together," added Ingebjörg.

Synnöve knew not what she should answer.

Sæmund looked over his shoulder at her. "Wait, and it will ring soon for you," said he.

Synnöve grew very red; her mother looked sharply up at him. But he smiled with his eyes fixed on her.

"It will be now as the Lord wishes; was not that what you said a while ago?" said he, and sauntered on in advance toward the church, the others following.

At the church door there was a crowd, and when they came to look it was not open. Just as they drew nearer to inquire into the cause of this, the door was opened, and the people poured in; but some of them stepped back, and this separated those who were entering. Up against the wall stood two people, in conversation, one of them tall and heavily built, with light but straight hair and snub nose; and this was Knud Nordhoug, who, when he saw the Granlid family approach, stopped talking, looked rather embarrassed, but stood still, nevertheless. Sæmund was obliged now to go right past him, and fixed on him a pair of eyes, as he did so; but Knud did not lower his either, although their gaze was not steady. Now came Synnöve, and the

moment she so unexpectedly caught sight of
Knud she grew deathly pale. Then Knud cast
down his eyes, and straightened himself up
from the wall to go. He had taken only a few
steps when he saw four faces turned to his;
these were Guttorm's, his wife's, Ingrid's, and
Thorbjörn's. As one bewildered, he went
straight toward them, so that without knowing what he was doing he soon stood face to
face with Thorbjörn himself; the latter at once
made a movement to turn aside; but several
people had come up, and this could not so easily be done. This occurred on the stone slab
lying outside of the Fagerlid church. Upon
the threshold of the vestibule Synnöve had
paused, and Sæmund farther in; as they stood
higher than the others, they could distinctly see
every one outside, and be seen by them. Synnöve had forgotten all else around her, and only
stared at Thorbjörn; the same with Sæmund,
his wife, the Solbakke couple, and Ingrid.
Thorbjörn felt this, and stood as one nailed to
the spot; but Knud thought he must do something here, and so he stretched out one hand

little way, but said nothing. Thorbjörn also
put his forward a little, but not so that the
two hands could touch.

" Thanks for " — began Knud, but remem-

bered at once that this was not the proper
greeting here, and drew back a step.

Thorbjörn looked up, and his eye fell on
Synnöve, who was as white as snow. With a
long stride forward and a vigorous grasp of
Knud's hand, he said, so that those nearest
could hear it, " Thanks for last, Knud ; we may
have gained much good from it, both of us."

Knud gave vent to a sound, almost like a sob,
and it seemed two or three times as though he
tried to speak, but the effort was in vain. Thorbjörn had nothing further to say, he waited,
did not look up, — only waited. There was uttered, meanwhile, not a word ; and as Thorbjörn
now stood there twirling his hymn-book, it
chanced that he dropped it. At once Knud
stooped, picked it up, and handed it to him.

" Thank you ! " said Thorbjörn, who had half
stooped himself. He raised his eyes, but as
Knud looked down again, Thorbjörn thought,
" It is best for me to go." And so he went.

The others went, too, and when Thorbjörn
had been seated for a while, and ventured to
look over at the women's pew, his gaze met
Ingebjörg's face, beaming with a motherly smile
on him, and that of Karen Solbakken too, whc
evidently had been waiting for him to look over
there ; for the moment he did so she nodded

at him three times, and when he hesitated she
nodded again three times, still more gently
than before. Sæmund, his father, whispered in
his ear, " I thought so." They had heard the
opening prayer, sung a hymn, and the confirmation candidates were already taking their places
before he whispered to him the next time :
" But Knud does not know much about being
good ; let it ever be far from Granliden to
Nordhoug."

The confirmation began by the priest coming
forward and the children uniting in singing
Kingo's confirmation hymn. To hear them sing
all at once and without accompaniment, their
fresh young voices so full of trusting hope, is
calculated to touch people, and especially those
who are not too far advanced in life to remember their own day. When after this deep silence ensues, and the priest, the same now as
more than twenty years ago, the same who has
taken such pains to find an occasional little
hour wherein he has talked for the improve-
ment of every single one of them, — when now
he clasps his hands over his breast and joins in
the hymn, there is indeed much emotion. But
the children begin to shed tears when the priest
talks of their parents, and wishes them to pray
to the Lord for their children. Thorbjörn, who

but recently lay at the point of death, and still
more recently believed that he would be an invalid all his life, wept much, but especially
when the children took upon them their vow,
and all seemed so sure of being able to keep it.
He did not once look over at the women's pew,
but at the end of the service he went over to
Ingrid, his sister, and whispered something to
her, whereupon he hurriedly pressed forward
and went out; and some were under the impression that he had gone up over the slope and
through the woods, instead of by the road, but
they were not sure of this.   Sæmund searched
for him ; gave it up, though, when he saw that
Ingrid too was gone.   He then looked round
for the Solbakke people; they were seeking
everywhere for Synnöve, whom no one had
seen.   Then they started for home, each separately, and without their children.

But already far on their way were both Synnöve and Ingrid.

" I am almost sorry that I came along," said
the former.

" It is no longer serious now that father
knows of it," said the latter.

" Yes, but he is not *my* father," replied Syn
növe.

" Who knows ? " replied Ingrid; and then
they said nothing more upon that subject.

" This must be where we were to wait," remarked Ingrid, as the road made an abrupt
curve, and they entered a dense wood.

" He has taken a long, roundabout way,"
said Synnöve.

" Already come ! " interposed Thorbjörn ; he
arose from behind a great stone.

He had ready in his mind all that he wanted
to say, and that was not a little. But to-day
things could not go wrong ; for his father knew
his wishes and approved them, of which he felt
sure, after what had occurred at church. This
oportunity was what he had been longing for
the whole summer, and he surely would be
more able to speak now than he had ever been
before. " We had better take the road through
the woods," observed he ; " we will get on faster
that way." The girls said nothing, but went
with him. Thorbjörn thought about speaking
to Synnöve, but first he wanted to wait until
they got up over the hill, afterward until they
were across the marsh ; yet when they were
well across, he decided that it was best not to
begin until they had come into the woods, farther on. Ingrid, who probably thought they
were getting on pretty slowly, began to slacken
her pace, and fell more and more behind, until
she was scarcely visible. Synnöve pretended

she did not notice this, but began to pick here
and there a berry which thrust itself forward
on the roadside.

" It would be strange if I could not find words
for myself," thought Thorbjörn ; and so he remarked, " The weather proved to be fine to-day,
after all."

" So it did," answered Synnöve. And then
they walked on a piece again. She picked berries, and he kept moving.

" It was kind of you to come with me," said
he ; but to this she made no answer. " It has
been a long summer," he continued , but to
this she made no answer, either.

" No, as long as we are walking," thought
Thorbjörn, " we will never get the conversation started. I think we had better wait a little for Ingrid," said he.

" Yes, let us do so," answered Synnöve, and
stood still.

There were no berries here to stoop for, —
this Thorbjörn had plainly seen ; but Synnöve
had picked up a large straw, and now she stood
and threaded the berries on the straw.

" To-day I have been strongly reminded of
the time when we went together to confirma·
tion," said he.

" I, too, thought of it," replied she.

"Many things have happened since that time," said he ; and as she made no answer, he continued : " but most of them have been different from what we expected."

Synnöve was very industriously threading her berries on the straw, and held her head bowed down as she did so. He advanced a little in order to look into her face ; but, as though she observed this, she managed to make it necessary for her to turn again. Then he grew almost afraid that he should not be able to say what he desired.

" Synnöve, you must have something to say, too."

She looked up and laughed. " What shall I say ? " asked she.

He recovered all his courage, and wanted to put his arm right around her waist; but when he came near her, he did not exactly dare to do so. He therefore merely asked, very timidly, " Ingrid has talked with you, I presume ? "

" Yes," replied she.

" Then I dare say you know something, too," said he. She was silent. " Then I dare say you know something, too," he repeated, and drew nearer the second time.

" You know something, too, I suppose," answered she.

He could not see her face.

"Yes," said he, and tried to take hold of one of her hands; but she was more industrious now than ever. "It is so provoking," continued he; "you steal my courage away." He could not see whether she smiled to this, and therefore he did not know what he should add. "To cut the matter short," said he, suddenly, speaking in a loud tone, although the voice was not quite steady, "what have you done with that note?"

She made no reply, but turned away. He moved after her, laid one hand on her shoulder, and bent over her.

"Answer me," he whispered.

"I have burnt it."

He quickly seized hold of her and turned her toward him; but then he saw that she was about to cry, and so he did not dare to do anything but let go his hold of her again. "It is too bad that her tears come so easily," thought he.

Just at that moment she said, "Why did you write the note?"

"That Ingrid has told you."

"Yes, of course; but — it was hard in you.'

"Father wished that " —

"Nevertheless " —

"He believed that I would be a broken-down invalid all my life; hereafter *I* shall take care of you," said he.

Ingrid appeared at the foot of the hill, and they started at once to go on.

"It seemed as though I cared most for you when I no longer thought I should be able to get you," he continued.

"One knows one's self best when one is alone," said she.

"Yes; then we find out who has the greatest power over us," said Thorbjörn, in a clear voice, and walked gravely by her side.

She picked no more berries.

"Will you have these?" asked she, handing him the straw.

"Thank you!" said he, and held fast to the hand that reached him the berries. "So then it is best that things go on in the old way," said he, in rather a faint voice.

"Yes," she whispered, scarcely audibly, and turned away.

Then they went onward, and so long as she was silent he did not either dare touch her or speak; but he felt no weight at all in his body, and therefore came pretty near tumbling over. There was a burning in his eyes, and when, just then, they reached an elevation from which

Solbakken was plainly visible it seemed to him as though he had lived there all his life, and longed to get home.

"I might just as well go over with her at once," thought he; and, drinking in courage from the view, he grew stronger in his resolve with every step.   "Father will help me," thought he.   "I cannot bear this any longer; I must go over there, — I must!"   He walked faster and faster, looking straight before him; there seemed to be a glow over parish and gard. "Yes, to-day; not an hour longer will I wait;" and he felt so strong that he knew not which way he should turn.

"You are leaving me behind," he heard from a sweet voice just back of him.

It was Synnöve, who had scarcely been able to follow him, and now had to give up.   He felt ashamed, turned, and walked back with outstretched arms, thinking, "I will lift her right over my head;" but when he came near, he did not do so at all.

"I walk so fast," said he.

"You do," replied she.

They were near the parish road; Ingrid, who for some time had been out of sight, came up right behind them.

"Now you two shall not walk together any longer," said she.

Thorbjörn was startled at this; it came too soon for him. Synnöve became also a little embarrassed.

"I have so much I ought to say to you," whispered Thorbjörn. She could not avoid smiling. "Oh, well," said he, "another time" — and he took her hand.

She looked up with a clear, full gaze; he grew warm under it, and promptly it ran through his mind, "I will go with her at once!" Then she discreetly withdrew her hand, turned calmly to Ingrid, bade her farewell, and went slowly down toward the road. He was left standing behind.

The brother and sister went home through the woods.

"Did you now have a talk together?" inquired Ingrid.

"No, the road was too short," said he, walking fast, as though he did not want to hear more.

"Well?" asked Sæmund, looking up from his dinner, as the two entered the room. Thorbjörn made no reply, but went over to the bench opposite, probably to take off his things; Ingrid followed, laughing slyly. Sæmund began to eat again; now and then he looked over

at Thorbjörn, who seemed very busy, smiled,
and ate on. " Come and eat," said he ; " the
dinner will be cold."

" Thank you, I do not want anything," said
Thorbjörn, and sat down.

" So ?" and Sæmund went on eating. Presently he said, " You were in a great hurry to
get away from church to-day."

" There were some people we had to talk
with," said Thorbjörn.

" Well, did you get to talk with them ? "

" I scarcely know," said Thorbjörn.

" The deuce you do not ! " cried Sæmund, and
went on eating. Shortly after he finished, and
arose ; he walked over to the window, stood
a while looking out, then turned, and said,
" See here, let us go out and look at the
crops." Thorbjörn arose. " No, you might
as well put your coat on." Thorbjörn, who was
in his shirt-sleeves, laid hold of an old jacket
that hung above him. " You see, I have put
on a new one," said Sæmund. Thorbjörn did
the same, and they went out ; Sæmund leading
the way, Thorbjörn following.

They went down toward the road. " Shall
we not go over to the barley ? " asked Thor
björn.

" No, we will go yonder to the wheat," replied Sæmund. Just as they reached the road, a cart came slowly driving along. "That is one of the Nordhoug carts," said Sæmund.

"Yes, those are the young people from Nordhoug," added Thorbjörn. By the young people he meant the newly-married couple.

The cart halted as it came near the Granlid men. "She is really a proud woman, that Marit Nordhoug," whispered Sæmund, and could not take his eyes from her. She sat leaning back in the cart, with one kerchief loosely tied about her head, and another drawn around her. She was looking fixedly out at the two; there was not the slightest emotion in her clear-cut, strong features. Her husband was very pale and thin, had a still more gentle look than formerly, much as one who has a sorrow he cannot speak of.

"Are you men out looking at the grain?" asked he.

"It seems so," replied Sæmund.

"It is doing well this year."

"Oh, yes, it might have done worse."

"You are late," said Thorbjörn.

"There were a great many acquaintances to take leave of," said the man.

"Why — are you going on a journey?" asked Sæmund.

" I expect to, yes."

" Are you going far? "

" Oh, yes."

" How far, for example? "

" To America."

" To America! " exclaimed both men in a breath. " A new-married man! " added Sæmund.

The man smiled, and said, " 'I think I will stay here for the sake of my foot,' said the fox, when he had been caught in the trap."

Marit looked at him, and then at the others, and a slight flush overspread her face; otherwise it was unchanged.

" I suppose your wife will go with you?" said Sæmund.

" No, she will not, either.'

" They say it is easy to gain position in America," said Thorbjörn; he felt that the conversation should not be allowed to come to a stand-still.

" Oh — yes," said the man.

" But Nordhoug is a good gard," remarked Sæmund.

" There are too many people on it," replied the man. His wife looked at him again. " One stands in the way of the other,' he added.

"Well, good luck on your journey," said Sæmund, and took his hand. "The Lord grant you what you wish to find!"

Thorbjörn looked his old school-mate earnestly in the eye. "I will talk with you by and by," said he.

"It is good to have some one to talk with," said the man, and scraped the bottom of the cart with his whip.

"Do come over to our house," said Marit; and Thorbjörn, as well as Sæmund, looked up in surprise; they had really forgotten that she had so pleasant a voice.

They drove on; the cart moved slowly away; a little cloud of dust encircled them, — the evening sun fell directly on it; against his wadmal clothes her silken kerchief glistened. They came to a hill, and disappeared.

The father and son walked on for a long time before they said anything.

"I have a foreboding that it will be long before he returns," observed Thorbjörn, finally.

"That is best, I suppose," remarked Sæmund, "when one has not secured happiness at home;" and once more they walked silently on.

"You are going past the wheat field," said Thorbjörn.

"We can look at that on our way back," and they went farther on. Thorbjörn did not altogether like to ask where they were going; for they had now passed the Granlid grounds.

CHAPTER IX.

GUTTORM and Karen Solbakken had already finished their dinner when Synnöve, flushed and out of breath, entered.

" Why, my dear child, where have you been ? " asked her mother.

" I stayed behind with Ingrid," answered Synnöve, and remained standing, while she took off a couple of kerchiefs. Her father was searching in the cupboard for a book.

" What could you two have to talk about that took such a long time ? "

" Oh, not anything."

" Then it would have been better if you had kept with the church people, my child." Karen got up and placed Synnöve's dinner before her. When Synnöve had taken her seat at the table, and her mother had sat down directly opposite, the latter said, " I suppose there were others you were talking with."

" Yes, there were many," replied Synnöve.

" The child may surely be allowed to talk with folks," said Guttorm.

"To be sure she may," said the mother, rather more gently; "but still she ought to come home with her parents."

To this no reply was made.

"It was a blessed church day," remarked the mother. "It does me good to see the young folks come forward in church."

"It makes one think of one's own children," said Guttorm.

"You are right there," said the mother, and sighed. "No one can tell how things will go with them."

Guttorm sat silent for a long time. "We have much to thank God for," said he at last; "He has allowed us to keep one of ours."

The mother sat drawing her finger along the table, and did not look up. "She is our greatest joy," said she, softly; "and she has done well," she added, still more softly. There followed a long silence.

"Yes, she has given us much happiness," said Guttorm; and later, in a soft voice, "The Lord make her happy!"

The mother was still drawing her finger along the table; there fell now a tear upon it, which she kept wiping away.

"Why are you not eating?" said the father looking up, a little while later.

"Thank you, I have done," replied Synnöve.

"But you have not eaten anything," now spoke up the mother, too; "and you have had a long walk."

"I am not able to," said Synnöve, and busied herself with an end of her kerchief.

"Eat, my child," said the father.

"I cannot," said Synnöve, and burst into tears.

"But, dear, why are you crying?"

"I do not know," and she sobbed.

"She does cry so easily," said the mother.

The father got up and walked to the window. "There are two men coming up this way," said he.

"Why — is that so, at this time of day?" inquired the mother, and she too went to the window. They looked for a long time down the hill.

"Dear, who can it be?" said Karen, at last, but not quite as though she were seeking information.

"I do not know," replied Guttorm, and they stood and watched.

"Really, I cannot understand it," said she.

"Nor I either," said he.

The men came nearer.

"It must be they, nevertheless," said she, finally.

" Yes, I suppose so," said Guttorm.

The men came nearer and nearer. The elder of the two paused and looked back; the younger one did the same; then they continued onward.

" Can you imagine what they want?" asked Karen, in about the same way as the first time.

" No, I cannot," replied Guttorm.

The mother turned, went over to the table, removed the dishes, and cleared up a little. " You had better put on your kerchief, my child," said she to Synnöve; " for here come some strangers."

Scarcely had she said this before Sæmund opened the door and came in, Thorbjörn directly behind him. " Bless the company!" said Sæmund, paused a little at the door, then went quietly to greet those within; Thorbjörn followed. They came last to Synnöve, who still stood in a corner, with her kerchief in her hand, and did not know whether she should put it on or not; indeed, perhaps scarcely knew that she held it in her hands.

" Pray, be seated," urged the mistress of the house.

" Thank you; it is not far over here," said Sæmund, but sat down nevertheless. Thorbjörn took a seat by his side.

" We lost sight of you altogether at the church to-day," said Karen.

"Yes; I was looking for you," said Sæmund.

"There were many people there," said Guttorm.

"A great many," repeated Sæmund ; "and it was a fine church day, too."

"Yes, we were just talking about it," said Karen.

"A confirmation is a very touching sight to any one who has children himself," added Guttorm ; his wife moved a little on the bench.

"That it is," said Sæmund; "it sets one to thinking seriously about them ; and that is why I wandered over here this evening," he added, looking about him with an air of security, and he changed his quid of tobacco, laying the old one cautiously aside in his brass tobacco-box. Guttorm, Karen, and Thorbjörn, let their eyes wander in different directions.

"I thought I would accompany Thorbjörn over here," began Sæmund slowly; "it would take him a long time to get here alone, I fancy, — and he would make poor work of it, besides, I am afraid." He cast a sly look at Synnöve, who was conscious of it. "Now, it is just this way: he has set his heart on Synnöve from the time he was old enough to understand anything about such matters ; and it is not very sure but she also has set her heart on him. And so I think it is best for them to come together. I was little in favor of this in the days when I saw he was scarcely able to manage himself. to say nothing of other things, but now I think I can vouch for him; and if I cannot she can, for her power is now the greatest, I suppose. What do you two think of our making a match for them? There is no need of any haste, but I do not know, either, why we should wait. You, Guttorm, are pretty well off; I, to be sure, rather less so, and have more to divide among; but I fancy that will be all right. You will have to say now what you think of this, — I will ask her afterwards; for I am pretty sure I know what she wishes."

Thus spoke Sæmund. Guttorm sat in a stooping position; kept alternately placing his hands one above the other; made several signs to raise his head, each time drawing his breath more heavily, but did not succeed until the fourth or fifth time; then at last he straightened his back, stroked his knees up and down, looked over at his wife, so that the glance now and then took in Synnöve. The latter did not stir; no one could see her face. Karen sat drawing her finger on the table.

" The fact is — it is a fine offer," said she.

" Yes, and it seems to me we might as well

accept it with thanks," said Guttorm, in a loud voice, as though he were considerably relieved, and looked from her to Sæmund, who had folded his arms and leaned up against the wall.

"We have only this one daughter," added Karen; "we have to consider a little."

"There is reason in that," said Sæmund; "but I cannot see what objection there can be to giving an answer at once, as the bear said, — he had been asking the peasant whether he could have his cow."

"We might as well answer at once," remarked Guttorm, and glanced at his wife.

"What I thought was that perhaps Thorbjörn might be a little wild," said she, but did not look up.

"That, I think, has righted itself," suggested Guttorm; "you know yourself what you said to-day."

The husband and wife exchanged looks; this lasted probably a whole minute. "If we could only be sure of him," said she.

"Well," said Sæmund, joining in the conversation again, "so far as that matter goes, I can only say what I have said before; it is all right with the load when she holds the reins. It is astonishing what power she has over him; I had proof of that when he lay ill at home,

13

and did not know how things were going with him, — whether he would get well or not."

" You should not be so hard to please," said Guttorm. "You know what she wants herself, and you know it is for her we live ! "

Then Synnöve looked up for the first time, and turned a pair of large thankful eyes on her father.

" Oh, yes," sighed Karen, after a moment's silence; and now she drew her finger along the table a little more vigorously than before. " If I have held out against it the longest, it was because I meant well by it, I suppose. Perhaps I was not so hard as my words." She looked up and smiled; but the tears would come.

At this Guttorm arose. " Then, in God's name, that has come to pass that I have most wanted of all things in the world," said he, and crossed the floor to Synnöve.

" I have never doubted that," said Sæmund, also rising. " Those who are meant to come together come together." He crossed the floor.

" Well, what have you to say to this, my child ? " said the mother, she too going over to Synnöve.

She still kept her seat; the rest stood about her, all except Thorbjörn, who sat where he had first taken his place.

"You must get up, my child," whispered the mother to her; whereupon she arose, smiled, turned away, and wept. "The Lord be with you now and always!" said the mother, threw her arms around her, and wept too. The two men walked across the floor, each in his own direction. "You will have to go over to him," said the mother, still weeping, as she let go of her, and stole a loving glance at her.

Synnöve took a step forward; then stood still, because she could not get any farther Thorbjörn sprang up and went toward her, seized her hand, held it, knew not what more to do, and stood there holding it until she gently withdrew it. Then they stood silent by each other's side.

The door opened noiselessly; a head was thrust into the room. "Is Synnöve there?" was asked, in a cautious voice; it was Ingrid Granliden.

"Yes, she is here; come in!" cried the father. Ingrid seemed to hesitate a little. "Come now; all is well here," he added. They all looked at her.

She appeared rather embarrassed. "There may be somebody else outside," said she.

"Who is it?" inquired Guttorm.

"It is mother," replied she, softly.

" Let her come in ! " said four voices at once.

And the Solbakken wife went to the door, while the others exchanged pleased glances.

" You may as well come in, mother," they heard Ingrid say. And so Ingebjörg Granli· den, in her glittering head gear, entered.

" I knew what was going on," said she, " although Sæmund never can tell anything. And so Ingrid and I could not help coming over here."

" Yes, it is just as you want it to be here," said Sæmund, and moved so that she might approach.

" God bless you for drawing him over to you ! " said she to Synnove, putting her arm about her neck, and patting her. " You have been very faithful, my child ; it has ended after all as you desired," and she stroked her cheek and hair. Her tears ran down over her face ; she paid no heed to these, but carefully wiped away Synnöve's. " Yes, it is a fine boy you are getting," added she, " and now I feel perfectly safe about him," and she embraced her once more.

" I tell you, mother has found out more in her kitchen about this matter," said Sæmund, " than we others who have been right in the midst of it."

The weeping and emotion were calming down a little. The housewife began to bethink her of the evening meal, and spoke to little Ingrid about helping her, " for Synnöve is not fit for it this evening." And so Ingrid and she set to work to cook the cream-porridge. The men got to talking about that year's harvesting, and what its results might be. Thorbjörn had taken his seat by the window, and Synnöve glided over to him and laid her hand on his shoulder.

" What are you looking at ? " she whispered

He turned his head, gave her a long, tender look, then directed his gaze out of the window again. " I am looking over at Granliden," said he ; " it seems so strange to look at it from here."